Terror by Day

A Patrick Dawlish Mystery

John Creasey *writing as* Gordon Ashe

OPEN ROAD
INTEGRATED MEDIA
NEW YORK

ISBN: 978-1-5040-9878-6

This edition published in 2025 by Open Road Integrated Media, Inc.
180 Maiden Lane
New York, NY 10038
www.openroadmedia.com

TERROR BY DAY

CHAPTER I

MR. DAWLISH PROTESTS

Dawlish would not, he admitted frankly, have liked to be a policeman; and yet there were times when the very Fates appeared determined to make him one, or as near as made no difference. He made this remark bitterly on a fine spring morning to no less a person than his old friend, Chief Inspector Trivett of Scotland Yard, who called, spruce and immaculate and yet troubled, at his Brook Street flat. It was a newly-rented flat, and Trivett had not been there before; instead of admitting his appreciation of it, he said abruptly:

"Dawlish, are you busy just now?"

Dawlish, who at six feet one inch topped Trivett by two inches, was a large man, and but for a broken nose he would have been handsome. The early sun—early for him: it was ten o'clock—contrived to find a way into Brook Street and his lounge, where a shaft shone on his fair hair, the thick lines of his eyebrows, and the blue, clear and wide-set eyes, which at times had a disconcertingly direct stare. The broken nose was generous, yet did not seem out of place, for his features were large and there was a ruggedness about his square, grooved chin, his full lips parted

3

over large white teeth. A big man, impressive in loose-fitting silver-grey which did justice to his figure and his tailor.

"Precisely what do you mean by busy?" he demanded now.

Trivett frowned. "Pat, if you were told we were up against large-scale crime, what would you think the most likely type just now?"

Dawlish hesitated, knowing that Trivett was serious, then said slowly:

"Didn't I hear a whisper about a drive against drugs back in September?"

"It was true enough." Trivett watched as Dawlish mixed whisky-and-soda, making no comment about the early hour for spirits. "We cleaned up most of the known or suspected channels, and for a few weeks there was a definite decrease in the stuff. Now, it's flooding the market, and we can't find where it's coming from. Cocaine and heroin and opium are far too prevalent. Particularly in your set."

"I'm a man of the world, not Mayfair," Dawlish grinned. "Have a drink—it'll cheer you up. Isn't Gulliver your specialist on the stuff?"

"Thanks." Trivett drank. "He was, yes. He had a nasty crack in September; some of the gentry made a fight of it, and Gulliver's heart isn't too good. On medical advice he's off the active list— oh, he's still at the Yard, but little more than a passenger, which doesn't please him at all." Trivett smiled a little, although not altogether in amusement. "One way and the other we're so busy that we don't know which way to turn. Pat—I was talking to the A.C. this morning. You were mentioned."

Dawlish eyed him cautiously: Sir Archibald Morely, Chief of the Criminal Investigation Department, was not a man to talk lightly and for the sake of talking.

"I," he said with mock severity, "am not a drug-trafficker, nor taker, nor investigator."

"Oh, don't be an ass. Will you keep your eyes open for anything that might give us some help? I know you're not anxious to go into it again, but—"

"On the occasions when I have been in 'it'," said Dawlish gently, "it has not been approved for a long time. In fact, you've been obstructive where you could be, which isn't meant personally. And why should I risk wind and limb and neck, for that matter, doing a job which isn't mine?"

"You'd be doing something useful instead of taking other men's girls out to lunch. And probably you won't be risking anything."

"That wasn't said with conviction." Dawlish smiled. "Worried, old man?"

"I am—in fact, we are," admitted Trivett. "There's a youngster at the Foreign Office who's been selling minor secrets, his payment being mostly in 'snow'. The cover-up was damned efficient; we got at two of his suppliers, but then met a blank wall. Awbridge, the Third Under-Secretary at the Admiralty, has been off-colour for some days; cocaine again, although he swears he hasn't taken it knowingly; we're trying to find out how it's been administered. Anyhow, that gives you an idea how serious it might be?" He broke off expectantly, and Dawlish nodded.

He was well aware of the trust implied by Trivett's statement, knew that the Yard was always reluctant to call on anyone for assistance unless it be a pathologist or a technical expert. In short, it was a compliment rarely bestowed—and yet he was not sure that he appreciated it.

He was not possessed of any driving urge to investigate crime, which only made it the more annoying that he had twice been highly successful in doing so. No small affairs either, as he readily admitted: Pat Dawlish was no victim of false modesty.

There had been the first, when he had hauled a live thief through his window, to find him dead by the time he was properly in the room; that had been at the home of Sir Jeremy Pinkerton, his maternal uncle and one of his few relatives. The personal element had been considerable, too, in the second affair, when one of London's lovelies had appealed to him for help.

Trivett was not one of London's lovelies.

But Trivett was doing something that obviously he hated, asking what amounted to a favour of someone he knew would be reluctant to grant it, while breaking an unwritten law of the C.I.D. Trivett was patently uncomfortable—and he had presented a strong case.

Dawlish wrinkled his forehead.

"Is it official? The request, I mean?"

"If you want it so, yes. Preferably, we'd like you to keep your eyes open. We'll give you all the help you need, of course, but—"

"If I come a cropper, the Yard preserves its unsullied record," said Dawlish. "I know. It sounds suspiciously like passing the buck."

"It isn't. We're worried, and we need someone moving in—"

"Say it. My 'set', whatever that may mean."

"Someone who can gain entry to various places without arousing suspicion," said Trivett equably. "As you can. For instance, two night-clubs have a large proportion of addicts: the Night Templar and the Black Out. Know them?"

Dawlish raised his brows.

"Indeed I do . . . Nothing doing as far as your men are concerned?"

"No, it all seems straightforward at both places, but—" Trivett shrugged.

"A nice, convenient little word, 'but'," said Dawlish. "All right. But no promises—and it might be a fizzle, you know."

"We'll risk that," Trivett seemed confident. "Don't run your head into too much danger."

"My game, my rules," Dawlish told him. "By the way, I've let my licence for a lethal weapon lapse; fix it for me, will you? I can supply the guns and ammunition."

Trivett chuckled. "You're on a drug hunt, not a man-hunt."

"Now wouldn't it be strange," said Dawlish gently, "if they should happen to coincide?"

CHAPTER II

MR. CUNNINGHAM IS PERTURBED

Into the orbit of Pat Dawlish, some two hours after he had talked with Trivett, came Mr. Andrew Cunningham. There was little surprising in that, for they were members of the Carilon Club, and also habitués. Cunningham was a tall young man—five years Dawlish's junior—somewhat lean and a trifle melancholy on the mornings after. His face, long and lean, lent itself to melancholy, as did his brown eyes, so large and faithful and at times appealing, although he objected to being told they were like a doe's.

Andy Cunningham's one claim to fame was his record of engagements. His repertoire included film actresses, stage-stars, one chorus girl, an Austrian countess, and an American heiress. With them all, Andy remained good friends. It was rumoured, about the time that he encountered Dawlish in the smoking-room of the Carilon, that he was contemplating his eighth or ninth engagement, this time to the daughter of a little-known peer. The daughter was also little-known; a surprising thing, since Andy usually chose a celebrity.

He was sitting in one of the enormous chairs with a paper

on his knees; smoking a cigarette and staring dolefully out of the window. All he could see was the tops of trees in St. James's Park, hardly the sort of thing to attract his attention.

"Could you," said Dawlish, beside him, "be sad about something, Andy?"

Cunningham had not seen Dawlish approaching, but he showed no surprise as he eyed the large man sorrowfully.

"I could." His voice was deep but it was not kept low, as the rules of the smoking-room demanded. "What is more, I am."

Four papers rustled, and four pairs of old eyes glared towards the speaker—to all of which Cunningham was oblivious.

"No lunch engagement?" demanded Dawlish.

"Two, as a matter of fact—I haven't decided which one to cut." Cunningham scowled, dubbed out his cigarette, and rose. "I'm going to have a drink; come and help me."

"Drink or decide?"

"Both." Ignoring the glared protests of the members, they strolled out and downstairs to the bar, where one could talk in a normal voice and not be frowned upon. "All joking apart, Pat, I'm in a jam. You know I'm engaged to Betty?"

"I did hear rumours, yes."

Cunningham grinned.

"Nicely put. Well, it's more than a rumour, and between you and me it's serious. That girl is—well, we won't take up all the time talking about Betty. She's just taken hold of me and shown me what a damned fool I was in the past and—" Cunningham, for him, was intensely serious—"let me tell you, Pat: if anything goes wrong between Betty and me, I just shan't give a damn for anything."

"Need anything go wrong?"

"I suppose, it needn't, but I can't expect even Betty to be angelic about everything, can I? Everything was all right until

Chloë cropped up again." As they reached the bar Cunningham ordered a large beer for Dawlish and a sidecar for himself then straightened his tie in the mirror behind it. "I was fond of Chloë," he admitted, "but between you and me, I don't think she would have said 'yes' if she hadn't been tight. I know I wouldn't have asked her, but you know how it is. Anyhow, we parted good friends and all that, about a couple of months ago, and I've seen her a dozen times since and everything's been friendly and smiling. And now," went on Andy Cunningham sorrowfully, "she rings me up and asks me to have lunch with her. Says she wants to talk to me seriously and she doesn't know anyone else who'll do. I mean, what else could I say but 'yes'? After all," added Andy ingenuously, "I thought Betty would be out of town."

"*Thought?*" Dawlish echoed.

"Well, I got the weeks mixed up," said Cunningham miserably. "I thought Betty would be away this week. Instead of that it's next week, and I'm due to lunch with her at the Regal, and Chloë at the Superb. If I let Betty down she's bound to find out why, and if I let Chloë down she might raise a stink. She's fiery, you know. Worst of it is, she sounded a bit flurried and whatnot over the 'phone yesterday; wanted to see me right away, but I was engaged." He finished his sidecar and ordered another. "I wish I'd had beer. Well, there it is. I don't mind telling you that if I thought it would work, I'd ask you to tackle Chloë for me, but it's impossible. I thought she was settling down, too; she's been with Morrell at the Black Out every night for a month."

Dawlish stirred. "Where?"

"The Black Out," said Andy gloomily. "Just about what I feel at the moment, old man. Blacked right out, polished right off. I suppose I'll have to toss for it."

"Don't play the fool," Dawlish urged. "Keep your appointment with Betty—I'll handle Chloë."

"You'll handle *Chloë*? Hang it, you don't know what you're letting yourself in for!"

Dawlish did.

Chloë Farrimond had made a hit in musical comedy at the tender age of seventeen. She was now nearly thirty, although she did not look her age. She was tiny and very lovely—but with red hair and all that is supposed to go with it. Her temperament was abhorred by every manager in London who ever put on a musical comedy, but the competition for her services was always fierce. The public raved over her. Hollywood agents tried to bribe her into films with fantastic contracts—and failed. Chloë was not so much in the news as the news itself.

It was absurd, thought Dawlish, to commit himself to Chloë for that lunch-time, and for Andy alone, he might not have made the sacrifice. But he was interested in the Black Out Club and also—more subconsciously than otherwise—the fact that she had been 'flurried and whatnot.' Dawlish had a sudden vision of Trivett and grinned at the thought of the Chief Inspector's predictable reaction to what could be called a hunch. Trivett had great faith in systematic investigation.

"What time's the appointment?" he asked Cunningham.

"One-fifteen."

"And Chloë is always late," said Dawlish. "I'll be there on the dot, and she'll have no complaints about that. Go and eat with your Betty, little man, and brood over the iniquities of deception. Oh, and there's one other thing—are you by any chance a member of the Black Out?"

"I'll say. Founder member, what's more."

"Well, I want to be one," Dawlish told him, "and I'm thinking of going along there tonight."

"I'm taking a party," said Cunningham promptly, "Betty's

crazy about night-clubs—it's a thing I'll have to cure her of. I'll be there around ten; just ask for me and they'll let you in. Who'll you be with?"

"I'm not sure yet," said Pat. "Thanks, old man. I'll be drifting."

The Superb was in Shaftesbury Avenue, and the club in Pall Mall, which meant a fifteen minutes' walk if he took it leisurely. He was pensive as he strolled along. Drugs were not pleasant things. Helping to stop their distribution might be no easy task, but certainly one worth while. He smiled sombrely, for he saw no reason why he should be able to stop it, it was his habit in all things to take them, as they came, rarely planning any campaign. Trivett's faith and that of the Assistant Commissioner was a pleasing thing but probably unfounded. Perhaps more than anyone else Dawlish realised that an ability to act fast and think afterwards had seen him through many a difficulty. And he had been lucky. . . .

He reached the splendid foyer of the Superb at ten past one and was acknowledged by the reception clerk and two commissionaires, but saw no acquaintances about. He was prepared to wait for fifteen minutes, before seeing Chloë, and picking up a magazine, was soon absorbed in a political essay. Finished, he glanced at his watch—to find that it was twenty to two.

Frowning, he hoisted his large body from the easy chair. The nearer commissionaire eyed him expectantly.

"Has Miss Farrimond been in?" Dawlish asked him.

"No, sir. Not yet, sir." If it was in the power of a commissionaire to wink imperceptibly, this one did.

Dawlish smiled to himself, realising that Chloë's habits were well known.

And then for the first time he saw the man in grey.

Most men could wear grey and pass quite unremarked. This man was noticeable. His suit, of good cut, was of clerical grey so was his tie. His white shirt showed little for the V of his waist-coat was shallow. His hair was grey: a peculiar shade of grey that matched his clothes. And he had grey eyes—unusual, slate-grey eyes.

Dawlish picked up these facts in a quick, comprehensive glance, and then returned to his chair. He was not, however, to be allowed to read another article. A shadow came between him and the window and as he glanced up the man in grey said drably:

"Excuse me, sir, you were asking for Miss Farrimond?"

"That's right."

If Dawlish was suddenly interested beyond the merits of the question, he did not show it.

"I am afraid, sir—" the colourless voice suited the man perfectly; it was devoid of expression and of accent, it was low-pitched and monotonous—"that Miss Farrimond has been unavoidably detained. She is, however, particularly anxious to see you."

Dawlish experienced a moment of sharp irritation: the man talked as if he were conjugating verbs in a little-known tongue. But he felt his interest quickening, for this grey man—a man of more than medium height although somehow he looked shorter—was not the type normally to be associated with Chloë.

"Where?" he asked.

"At her flat, sir, in de Mond Street. Will it be asking too much of you to come with me?"

"I don't think so," said Dawlish easily. "Although I hope she will find me some lunch. Isn't she well?"

"I have no information to the contrary, Mr. Cunningham but you will doubtless be able to know from her at first-hand."

It was almost impertinence, decided Dawlish, but he did not say so. The use of Andy's name reminded him that he was being taken for that careless swain, and he was also reminded of the fact that Chloë was not likely to be pleased with a substitute. That could be risked: for Chloë to send a messenger instead of dropping the appointment without a second thought was proof enough that she really wanted to see Andy.

He followed the grey man to a car; a Jaguar that gleamed new and brilliant in the sun. There was a chauffeur waiting, who opened the door with alacrity.

And then Pat Dawlish had the first shock of the affair of Chloë. For in the big limousine was another man dressed in grey; as nondescript to look at as the first—except that he was smiling, and in his right hand was an automatic, fitted with a Maxim silencer.

"Come in, Mr. Cunningham," he invited. "I am most anxious to talk with you. Please do not be disturbed. I shall not—I hope—need to use this."

He waved the gun in Dawlish's face, as the second man half-pushed him into the car, then joined him without a word. The chauffeur was already at the wheel, and the Jaguar moved swiftly into the stream of traffic in Piccadilly. The first movement caused Dawlish to sit down abruptly and he saw at once that the curtains of the car were drawn. The face of the man with the gun seemed more shadowy than ever, but the gun itself was motionless.

Dawlish wondered what would happen when it was learned that Andrew Cunningham was a mile or more away.

CHAPTER III

WHY?

To Dawlish, the most absurd thing of that mad few minutes was that gun in the stranger's hand. His garb was so distinctly clerical that it was like being held up by a reverend gentleman; it was impossible to believe that the gun might be used.

"You dislike talking, perhaps," said the man suddenly.

Dawlish rubbed his chin, and surreptitiously felt with his elbow for the hard lump of his own automatic. It was still there, and he blessed the whim that had made him pocket it before coming out.

"I'm allergic to surprises," Dawlish said. "It causes vocal paralysis—but it doesn't last long, as you see."

In the gloom, the other's face seemed pale and worried; his expression was in keeping with his clothes. He even glanced down at the gun in his hand, but he retained his grip. "I'm glad it doesn't last long, for I have several questions to ask you, and it would be most unfortunate if you were tongue-tied."

"I don't doubt it," said Dawlish, "but couldn't they have been asked without this—er—performance?"

The man in grey did not answer immediately, but considered Dawlish gravely.

"It is strange," he said at last. "You talk with a spontaneity that I was not led to expect. I believed you would be more easily frightened. You aren't frightened, are you?"

"What of?" asked Dawlish, and felt more at ease.

The other laughed: it was a strange, soft sound and it did not ring true, although doubtless he was amused.

"The gun, Mr. Cunningham."

"I was taught," said Dawlish gently, "to be afraid of the man behind the gun instead of the gun itself. I find I can't be, Mr.—"

"My name is Grey."

Dawlish had a shock, although he admitted that he should not have had. The pause after the 'Mr.' had been one of the simplest of try-ons, and he had expected no answer at all. The 'Grey', so obviously right, startled him, but did not rob him of his poise. He was consciously clinging to that, for the uncanny silence of the man who had brought him from the foyer, added to the strange passiveness of the man with the gun, was disturbing.

He saw through the windscreen that the car had turned off at Grosvenor Place, and that they were now travelling towards Victoria. Chloë Farrimond's flat was near the Station; *could* they be going to see Chloë?

"Thank you, Mr. Grey. And this gentleman—?" He lifted a hand to indicate the third occupant of the car, and Mr. Grey inclined his head.

"Also Grey. He is my brother."

"I've always wanted a brother," Dawlish murmured.

"I'm so glad you are friendly," said Mr. Grey. "I had been told to expect you to be startled at first, and then somewhat—er—boisterous. Obviously it is impossible to judge what a man's reaction when in danger is likely to be. You *are* in danger, you know." He added the last sentence gently, as if apologising for the reminder, and Dawlish found it difficult not to laugh.

"We'll let that pass," he said. "You may be right, but I'm sorry I've disappointed you. Dare I ask what you want?"

"I'm afraid not," said Mr. Grey, and he seemed really apologetic. "That subject must be deferred, but not for long. Now I want to give you some instructions. We shall reach Miss Farrimond's flat very shortly, and you will leave the car on your own. I shall sit inside, with the door open, and there will be someone else watching not far away. You will go straight into the building, where Miss Farrimond's flat is on the ground floor—but I need not give you those details; you will be well-acquainted with them. Should—" Mr. Grey's voice sank low, and yet held a sharp note that was almost of menace, and its contrast to his earlier tone sent a shiver down Dawlish's spine—"should you be foolish enough *not* to go straight in, I shall have to shoot you. It will be inconvenient, but necessary."

Dawlish stared: "My dear man, are you mad?"

"You would be surprised," said Mr. Grey unexpectedly. "Follow those instructions carefully, Mr. Cunningham. You will be told what to do inside the flat. Do it, or—" he shrugged—"it will be so unfortunate. Death is so very final. Don't, please, misunderstand me: I am quite serious."

Dawlish had no doubt of it. He told himself that if he managed to get away with a whole skin—and certainly he had not given up the hope of doing so—he would travel in future with a chain waistcoat.

It flashed through his mind that Andy would have acted much as the other had expected in the same circumstances; and from that it was not a far jump to ask *why* Cunningham should be subjected to this. The solemn-faced man with the dry sense of humour—a little weather-beaten that morning—could surely not have manoeuvred him into this?

He refused to believe that Chloë had sent for him this way and yet they were outside the block of luxury flats where London's loveliest termagant had two ground floor apartments knocked into one. In a daze, he moved towards the door, which Mr. Grey's brother opened obligingly, and as he stepped out he heard Grey's voice:

"Be *very* careful, Mr. Cunningham."

Dawlish hesitated for a moment on the pavement. He glanced right and left, and saw three pedestrians, all men, all of whom might be watching. There was one car, a small one, drawn up outside the main entrance, but no porter was in sight.

He stepped forward. Had there been a reasonable chance of a breakaway he doubted whether he would have taken it, for he wanted to know more—very much more. He was trying to believe that this affair could be associated with Trivett's vague suspicions of the Black Out Club, yet that was surely asking too much of the long arm of coincidence.

To believe in the affair at all was to suspect his mental balance. He was on a stretch as he entered the spacious hallway, where the walls were designed in futurist fashion in streaks of red, green, and yellow. There was no porter's room at the front. De Mond Mansions were far too exclusive to permit of that, and a bell invited one to ring for 'inquiries'. Dawlish ignored the invitation and stepped to the only door in sight, ten yards inside the hallway. Before tapping, he looked through the open front door and glimpsed Mr. Grey, drab and colourless in the tonneau of the Jaguar.

He tapped.

The door opened almost before his hand had left the tiny knocker, but he saw no one in front of him. From behind the door a sharp voice said:

"Come in."

Dawlish stepped in. The door was closed and a man stepped from behind it; Dawlish found it a relief that he wore a suit of Harris tweed. But the face of the wearer was more in keeping with the activities of Grey. It was a florid, beetle-browed face, with the eyes set too deeply and too close together, a short nose, and lips which could not properly close over prominent and yellow teeth. The man had his right hand in his coat pocket.

"Okay, no tricks now. Go straight through."

There was only one door, and Dawlish saw that it was ajar. More vividly than ever he felt the unreality of the situation; its clockwork precision did nothing to alleviate that feeling. This was Chloë's flat, occupied by at least one roughneck who seemed thoroughly at home, and who was obviously carrying out carefully planned arrangements. He was prepared to see anything when he went into the second room, from Chloë lying dead to Chloë standing in front of him with a gun. He was even prepared to find that it was a hoax, and he recalled uneasily that Andy Cunningham was renowned as a practical joker.

The room, Chloë's private lounge, did not hold Chloë.

Dawlish faced a man as tall as himself, and as broad across the shoulders. A man remarkable for the pallor of his face and the startling lustre of his blue eyes, which seemed exaggeratedly large and so brilliant that they looked feverish. It was like looking at a ghost of a man whose eyes alone were alive.

"Come in, Cunningham." A deep voice, holding a faint guttural note, seemed out of place from that pallid face, even though it suited the figure.

Pat pushed the door shut behind him, and saw that the man did not hold a gun. His hands were long, white and slim, the wrong hands for such a giant; Dawlish's were large and squarish, with a fine bunch of yellow hairs on the backs of the fingers. The fact that there was no gun, and the touch of his own against his thigh, gave him more confidence than he had felt since entering the car, and he said coolly:

"May I know what this tomfoolery is about?"

"You'll be well advised not to talk like that," said the pale-faced man. "Sit down, Cunningham—that's right. Now listen carefully. Two months ago Miss Farrimond gave you a present— a parting present, of a pair of silver-backed hair-brushes."

"So?" said Dawlish blankly.

"Where are they?" The question came sharply.

"On my dressing table, where else would you expect?"

The pale-faced man did not appear to relish sweet reason, for he barked:

"Don't lie! Your flat's been turned out twice—they're nowhere there."

"Oh," said Dawlish, still more blankly.

"When did you open them?" snapped the other, and this time Dawlish gaped.

"*Open* them? *Hair*-brushes?"

It was then that the affair changed from one of fantasy to fact, for the big man moved. He moved with a startling speed, quite deceiving Dawlish, who had no time to avoid the buffet which the clenched right hand gave him. It struck him in the neck, a tender spot, and it sent his head thudding back against the upholstery behind him. It dazed him; and yet it angered him. He was no longer filled with bemusing questions; he felt a cold rage against the striker, and with difficulty he kept his hands from clenching.

"Now perhaps you'll talk," said the other roughly. "I'm not here to waste time. The brushes, or—"

He did not say what he meant, but he conveyed it: and Dawlish was filled with a sudden fear which sent rage packing.

For from a shoulder holster a silenced Mauser had leapt into the other's right hand—while Dawlish, not being Cunningham, could not give any information.

And unless he did it seemed that he might die.

CHAPTER IV

ACTIVITY IN A FLAT

"The brushes, or—?" Dawlish echoed more gently than he felt. "My dear good man, if you tried for a year you wouldn't get those brushes. I'm not frightened, you know, nothing like so frightened as you are without them."

For a moment he thought he had miscalculated, for there was a savage anger in the fierce eyes; he seemed to see the finger trembling on the trigger. But in the same moment he realised that the retort had struck home, the brushes *were* of vital importance to the gunman: there was fear as well as anger in him.

Why should he go to such lengths to retrieve a parting gift from Chloë to Andy Cunningham?

"So you have guessed that," said the big man, clearly controlling his rage but none the less dangerous for that. "You are much cleverer than I had been led to believe, but not as clever as you imagine. Be advised, Cunningham, don't make me force you to talk, it would be painful."

"It would be impossible," said Dawlish. "You overrate yourself and your second-rate theatricals." He stood up as he spoke, and was not stopped: the gun was moved back two feet, so that it remained a yard from him. "Those brushes are quite safe and they'll remain quite safe."

"I—see." The words were simple, but not spoken pleasantly. The pale-faced man stepped to the wall, and his long hand sought for a bell-push; he did not move his eyes from Dawlish's. "Bilson has a way with him, Cunningham; others have proved obstinate." He touched the push but did not press. "I don't wish to make things unpleasant, believe me, and you've roused my curiosity. What made you put the brushes away?"

Pat grinned: "Let's call it sentiment."

"Cunningham, how much do you know?"

"How much could Chloë let out?" asked Dawlish easily. "Not much, but enough to make me think very hard. And you know I have never liked dope. Odd, isn't it?"

It was a long shot and he did not expect results. None the less he got them. If he had seen rage in the other's eyes before, he saw insensate fury in them now—and although the gun moved, although he knew the finger was trembling on the trigger, he felt a surge of exhilaration. This *was* part of the drug-racket; his half-formed association of Chloë's 'flurried and whatnot' state and the Black Out Club had not been groundless.

"You—"

"Be careful with that gun!" snapped Dawlish.

It was the simplest thing. He moved sharply to one side and half-turned, as if afraid of a bullet. Turning, he put his right hand inside his trousers pocket, gripping his own gun. He wasted no time, jerked it upwards inside the pocket, released the safety catch and fired, all while he was speaking. Firing, he moved again—and he saw the other man stagger, saw the gun fall from his right hand. The bullet had struck the barrel—

Dawlish leapt. He was on his man before the other had

recovered from the shock of the shooting. And Dawlish hit him: a piledriver with all the force in his great body.

The man staggered back, and his eyes rolled under the power of it. Dawlish flashed a left to his stomach—bringing him forward, chin thrust out. Then an uppercut with the whole force of his body behind it sent the man rocketing backwards.

He was still falling when Dawlish swung round towards the door. His knuckles were grazed but he was unaware of the pain as he went for his gun again. The door opened abruptly, as he expected it would. Bilson was not in sight; he clearly liked staying behind doors. Dawlish stepped to the wall where he could just see the door—and saw Bilson's right hand move slowly round, with the ugly snout of a silencer-fitted Mauser.

He fired.

The Mauser went flying and Bilson shrieked with pain as the gun was wrenched from his fingers. He jumped, too—into sight—and again Dawlish moved, with all the speed that made him a man to fear. He gripped Bilson's arm and dragged him into the room, then pushed him violently. Bilson struck the outstretched body of his employer and crashed heavily backwards, with barely time to realise what was happening.

Dawlish stood by the door, gun in hand, his expression bleak and expectant. He waited for perhaps thirty seconds. No sound came, there was no suggestion of others in the flat. There might be an interruption, of course; the shooting must have been heard.

His lips twitched as he suddenly remembered the spate of publicity two years before when Chloë had announced to the world that she was making her flat sound-proof because it was the only way she could sleep. With the doors and windows closed there was little chance the shooting had been heard outside.

The tables were turned, but he must make a decision quickly.

How much good would come from handing these men to the police? How much would the police be able to learn from them?

There was just one area where Dawlish believed he could improve on the police, and that was the fault of regulations and not policemen. 'My game, my rules,' he had told Trivett, and Trivett had known what he meant. He could exercise third degree far more effectively than the whole of the Yard put together.

But how could he get the men out of the flat?

He frowned suddenly. Why get them out of the flat? Thanks to Chloë's whimsy it was as good a place for operating as anywhere, provided there was no interruption from outside. As the thought flashed through his mind he glanced at the two men. The pale-faced gunman was lying with his eyes closed, his breathing stertorous; Bilson—an obviously nasty specimen— was licking his lips, not a little scared.

"Get up," Dawlish ordered.

Bilson hesitated, and Dawlish stepped forward and yanked him up by his coat-lapels.

"When I say move, *move*! Go through and lock and bolt the front door. I can see you from here, and I feel like more shooting." He shoved hard and Bilson staggered, regained his balance and hurried to the front door, a very frightened man. Dawlish watched the key turned in the lock and the bolts at top and bottom thrust home; and while the man's back was still towards him, reached down and turned up the bigger man's right eyelid. There was no twitching: the ferocity of his attack had paid off.

He frowned.

At the other's lips there was a faint bluish tinge, and the same thing was visible at his ears—remarkably small, pear-shaped, and very close to his head. The blueness perhaps showed more against the pallid skin than it would on a man of normal colour, but to Dawlish it spelt information; the fellow's heart was not sound.

Which explained the prolonged unconsciousness, and gave him time in which to work.

Bilson was coming back, his eyes avoiding Dawlish and his prominent teeth parted as he breathed noisily.

"Move faster," snapped Dawlish. "We're going to check the back entrance."

"It's—it's locked," muttered Bilson. "The boss told me to fix it before you came. I—"

"I'll check," said Dawlish. "Lead the way."

The next room, leading out of Chloë's boudoir, would be her bathroom, he reasoned rightly. The bathroom led into the bedroom, for he saw the double bed as Bilson opened the door.

And then Dawlish had a shock. For on the floor, stretched out unconscious, was Chloë herself.

He wasted no time in cursing himself for not realising that it was to be expected. As it was, he spent split seconds too long in staring at the actress, her lovely face colourless, her limpid eyes closed.

Was she breathing?

It was then that Bilson moved. He had picked up a chair and flung it before Dawlish realised what he was doing. He ducked, and as the chair went over his head, one leg striking his shoulder, Bilson leapt at him—and proved that he had courage.

Dawlish could have shot him.

He did not, but waited—and used the impetus of the other's rush to make his punch more telling. Bilson's chin was wide open, and the *crack*! of the punch echoed loudly, as he swayed back and crumpled up.

Dawlish glanced at his knuckles: they were bleeding, but not freely. Ignoring Chloë, he took the coverlet from the bed to bind Bilson's arms and legs. Then satisfied that he was safely immobilised, he stepped back into the dressing-room, forcing back a threatening panic about Chloë, who looked so still and so much like death.

The blue tinge on the 'Boss's' lips was no more pronounced, and for safety's sake Dawlish fastened his wrists with a necktie taken from the unconscious man. Finished, he went back to the bedroom.

He lifted Chloë easily. She was no weight: a small woman, inclined to a plumpness noticeable only because of her tiny frame. She was wearing a tailor-made costume and a white silk blouse, and in her pallor she looked sweet and innocent. There was a faint, subtle perfume about her, and he saw that in her clenched right hand there was a small, silver-mesh handbag.

She had, then, been about to leave the flat when she had been attacked. Confirmation of that came with the hat, a tiny thing of bottle-green like her costume, on the floor. He took in those details as he rested her on the bed, then felt for her pulse.

For a moment he seemed not to be breathing himself—then he relaxed as he detected the faint beat of the blood through her arteries.

He dropped her wrist and pulled back an eyelid. The point of the pupil was so small that it was barely visible, and the lips of Patrick Dawlish tightened.

There was no time for wondering whether she had been drugged into unconsciousness, or whether she made a habit of taking the filthy stuff. One thing was quite certain: he needed a doctor and he needed him quickly. But he also wanted to keep this thing as quiet as he could until after he had talked to the pale-faced man.

Thoughtfully he lifted the telephone and called the club. Bill

Farningham was due in town that day, time unspecified—but he would certainly make the Carilon his first stop. And Bill Farningham had been with Dawlish on the last occasion he and crime had fought.

As he heard the ringing tone, he wondered whether the luck would break his way.

And as he wondered, the two Mr. Greys, a little perturbed by the long silence, approached the front door of Chloë Farrimond's flat. . . .

CHAPTER V

ENTER BILL

"No, sir," said the clerk who answered Dawlish's call. "We have not yet seen Dr. Farningham, but we are expecting him any minute. We received a wire reserving a room and—er—a meal at two o'clock, sir."

"And it's now—"

"Nearly half-past, sir."

"My compliments to Dr. Farningham," said Dawlish, "and ask him to forgo his meal and come to see me at Miss Chloë Farrimond's flat in de Mond Street. The moment he arrives, you understand—provided it's before two-forty-five."

But as he replaced the receiver he wondered whether a delay of even half an hour might not be disastrous. He could so easily telephone Trivett and have a police surgeon on the spot within ten minutes.

Saving the pale-faced stranger for himself was only one reason why he did not.

Chloë had seemed worried, in Andy Cunningham's opinion, and Andy knew her too well to be deceived. Chloë, in short, might not appreciate the attentions of the police.

Apart from removing her shoes and assuring himself that she was wearing nothing tight about her waist, he left her as she was. In the next room, he found that the pale-faced man's eyes were flickering. He ignored that as he went through the other's pockets, taking out a wallet and a number of oddments that might be found in any suit. The man did not stir, although Dawlish knew that now he was aping unconsciousness.

The contents of the wallet offered nothing that seemed interesting on the surface. Unless an envelope, faintly blue, delicately perfumed, and addressed in feminine handwriting, could be termed interesting. The postmark was Victoria, and the envelope—quite empty—was addressed to:

Wilfrid Askew, Esq.,
18 Snow Court,
London, N.W.8.

"The St. John's Wood area," murmured Dawlish. "It might be the name of Pale-face here, although he doesn't look a Wilfrid. I'll attend to him, I think, when Bill and the others arrive."

He straightened up, but paused as the man on the floor spoke sharply:

"Cunningham!"

Dawlish turned.

"So you're awake," he said sardonically.

"What others?" snapped Pale-face.

"Was I speaking aloud? I do have friends, you know, and they can be quite—er—rough."

"The day will come when—"

"I'll regret it? I doubt it. Because I am going to make a nasty mess of you before handing you over to the police. That didn't occur to you, did it?"

"The police?" Again Dawlish saw fear in the other's eyes, and then the pale face hardened. "You damned fool! The woman will spend the rest of her life in gaol if you do that. Cunningham, it's time that you and I discussed this matter."

"Later, when I've reinforcements," said Dawlish. But he was seowling as he turned away. The talk of Chloë perturbed him, made him glad that he had refrained from going immediately to the police. Still, if Bill was coming, he—

Brr—brrr!

The ringing came from the front door and as he reached it, the bell rang twice again—so sharply that it made him jump. He slipped his right hand into his pocket, about the butt of his gun. He was prepared to find one of the Greys, although it was as likely a caller for Chloë: he was already wondering where her maids had gone.

He opened the door—

He saw both Greys—

The man who had talked in the car was first, and he held his right hand forward, then lifted it. Dawlish darted back, but he could not evade the small glass phial that burst in his face. He felt the biting sharpness of ammonia in his eyes and nose and could not prevent the spasmodic movement of his hands to his eyes—a movement that was fatal although already he had been outwitted. A foot caught him in the groin and he went reeling backwards, agony about him, helpless and defenceless.

"See to the others, Jonathan, I will look after him."

The man who had thrown the phial looked distastefully but without rancour at Dawlish, who was on the floor with his knees drawn up to his stomach and his hands covering his face.

Jonathan Grey hurried in to the two men and his brother hauled Dawlish towards a chair, but found him too heavy to lift.

There was a vague, satisfied smile on the senior Grey's face. But Dawlish did not see it.

Dawlish was aware of nothing but the burning blindness in his eyes and the ache in his groin. Lancelot Grey went through to where the pale-faced man was now sitting back in an easy chair, drinking a whisky-and-soda, as Jonathan busied himself releasing Bilson.

"Exactly what happened, sir?" asked the elder Grey.

"Cunningham was too quick," the pale man said gruffly. "He turned the tables—I must admit it was smart. It's lucky you came when you did, how did you get in?"

"I rang twice." Jonathan Grey looked smug. "And there was no answering signal. I knew that something was wrong and I used one of those little ammonia phials. So useful, sir, although you considered them childish."

"All right; never mind that now. Cunningham used the telephone—others may be coming. Get the woman out of here quickly. And can you handle Cunningham?"

"He will be difficult; he's a considerable weight."

"Then put him away."

"The—brushes, sir?"

"We'll have to leave them. He's too dangerous to leave here: he's seen you two as well as me, and he's no fool. Understand—" his voice rasped, his eyes seemed more feverish than when Dawlish had seen him first—"put him away. I'm taking no chances."

"Of course, sir. The flat will need tidying up; we should be able to make it look like—" he hesitated and his grey eyes widened. "I was going to say suicide, but with the woman missing and her ex-lover dead in her flat, it would be strongly circumstantial."

"Has she a gun?"

"She will doubtless have something to kill him with," said Lancelot Grey, with a cold smile.

The big man stood up, peered at himself in the mirror, and scowled. "I'm going right away. Bilson's to follow to Sunningdale as soon as he can." Cautiously, he fingered the contusion where Dawlish's fist had struck him, winced, then turned and left the room.

He was entering the small car which Dawlish had seen parked outside the block of flats when a Rover turned into de Mond Street with Dr. William Farningham at the wheel. Dr. Farningham was frowning. His dark, unruly hair needed attention; his homely, good-humoured face was set in a scowl, and he was secretly cursing Pat Dawlish. In cursing, he passed the entrance to de Mond Mansions. The pale-faced man waited long enough to be sure of that and then turned the corner. As he turned, Bill Farningham stopped, complained aloud of his carelessness, and reversed into the drive.

Out of the car he proved to be a shorter man than the average, stocky and broad-shouldered. He hurried into the hallway, and as he started towards the door of No. 1 it opened.

From Chloë's flat stepped a man who clearly looked tough, whose nose was swollen, and whose right eye was closing rapidly. Also there was a red bump on his chin. Into Bill Farningham's mind there sprang a considerable question mark.

Pat was here, and there had been a rough-house.

The roughneck closing the door was distinctly not a type to be working with Pat Dawlish, and Farningham's suspicions were quickened. If the man was not for Pat, he was against—and if he was against and yet going free, that suggested trouble.

Bill watched as the man hurried out to the waiting Jaguar. The chauffeur joined him quickly and both men started back for the flat. Bill moved into the shadows of the passage leading to other flats, but turned in time to see the door open after he had heard two short rings. He fingered his revolver thoughtfully for a moment or two. Then suddenly determined, he went to the door, drew a deep breath and rang sharply, twice, as Bilson had done. Ringing, he drew his gun from its holster, and as he did so, the door opened.

Bilson's effort to bang the door failed. Farningham went through, the gun forcing a passage. He saw Dawlish stretched out on the floor, and a man who seemed nothing but a grey shadow standing in the communicating door with a small automatic in his hand—an automatic with the handle covered by a handkerchief.

"What the *hell*!" said Dr. William Farningham blankly.

And then he was visited by inspiration.

"Ted!" he yelled. "Percy! for the love of Mike—"

And then Bilson leapt at him.

Farningham did not hesitate. He fired, catching Bilson in the shoulder and sending him round with the force of the bullet. Then he ducked—and a bullet from the small automatic went over his head.

And then a shout came from outside the flat.

Farningham realised subconsciously that the shout saved his life, for he was off balance and could not have avoided a second bullet. But the grey man was eyeing the door. And as his brother came rushing from the bedroom, he snapped:

"Let's get out! Shoot them down, but get out!"

His voice was no longer colourless.

The chauffeur appeared as both the Greys rushed for the door. Bilson was on the floor and gasping with pain. As the door opened wider, Farningham caught a glimpse of a middle-aged man who saw the guns and promptly dropped to his knees. Lancelot Grey fired over his head, but was more concerned with getting out. His brother and the chauffeur raced after him, and by the time Farningham was outside and the middle-aged man had recovered himself, the Jaguar was moving off. It went fast and Farningham urged:

"See to my friend in there—I'm following."

He rushed for his own car—but as it moved the tyres flattened. The Greys had contrived to put a bullet in each of the two front wheels. Farningham swore, and saw the Jaguar swinging round the corner into Victoria Street.

He also saw a policeman hurrying towards him.

He had no idea what Pat Dawlish was doing, except that it was dangerous. And he knew that in the past, Pat had not appreciated undue attentions from the police: and thus he waited, glaring ahead of him as though he could commit murder.

"I heard—" the policeman was youthful and intent, and believed he had heard shooting. But he paused at the sight of Bill's thunderous expression. And was glad he had not voiced his opinion, as Bill said with an obvious effort to keep his temper:

"A blow-out—*two* blow-outs, enough to waken the dead. Would you ruddy well believe it, Constable?"

CHAPTER VI

RECRUITS

The Constable believed it.

He was a trifle disappointed that there had been no shooting, but he went—after offering to call at a garage and having his offer refused firmly and with thanks.

Bill blew out his cheeks as the man went off. Then forgot his scare with the policeman and his disappointment at losing the two grey men and the chauffeur in sudden concern for Pat Dawlish who had not looked his fittest. He hurried to the flat, found the door ajar, and closed it firmly as he stepped through.

Dawlish was sitting on an easy chair, and the middle-aged stranger was bathing his eyes with water. They were red and swollen and still burning. Pat felt, in tact, as if he were eating hot ice, with the same unknown quantity attacking his eyes. Farningham recognised the faintly acrid smell that hung about the room.

"Had an ammonia bath?" he inquired genially.

The middle-aged man presented a weather-beaten countenance with pleasant blue eyes, firm lips, a decided chin, and a military moustache that spelt 'Colonel' in every bristle. He was dressed in blue serge and carpet slippers, incongruous at that moment.

"Dare I inquire into this?" he asked mildly.

"No one can stop you inquiring," said Bill amiably. "I don't know the first thing myself, except that my friend sent for me in a hurry and he appeared to need help. Feel like talking, Pat?"

Dawlish attempted to speak, and made a sound that might have been 'no'.

"All right," said Farningham, "if you feel like that about it. I wonder if there's a spot of boric acid in the house—"

"*Co!*" gasped Dawlish, and waved wildly towards the open door leading to the boudoir.

They looked at him, puzzled.

Dawlish stood up abruptly, made his way to the communicating door and leaned against the framework for support. He was stiff and still pain-racked, and he was desperately worried about Chloë Farrimond. Standing there he pointed to the next door, and Farningham went through.

He exclaimed: "Chloë, good God!" and Dawlish was left on his own as the stranger followed him into the bedroom.

"All right, I'm a doctor," Farningham told him. "Try to find that boric acid for my friend's eyes, will you? A little sugar and water held in his mouth will help, too. I'll look after Miss Farrimond. He knelt by the side of the bed and made the same quick examination as Dawlish had done, and—reached the same conclusions. He was able to diagnose, provisionally, that she had been drugged with one of the lesser poisons, and that the effect was not likely to be fatal.

He put an eiderdown over her and went back to Dawlish, whose face was being bathed again and was looking less puffy. It was ten minutes before he felt anything like himself, however, and by that time the stranger had introduced himself as Colonel Adams, tenant of the next door flat.

"Look here," he said, "this matter must be reported."

"Reported? To—oh, you mean the police." Bill looked at Dawlish, who found his voice properly for the first time.

"Special Branch, Scotland Yard," he said. He did not look at Bill: "There will be a full report on this, Colonel Adams, but for the time being your discretion would be appreciated."

Adams laughed, and smoothed his close-cut grey hair.

"Please, gentlemen. I'm not well-known, but I do know Pat Dawlish. After all, you've been in the headlines quite a bit, and—" he broke off, and shrugged. "Frankly, I think the police should know about this, but if you've any particular reason for any other course—"

He broke off, and his silence was an invitation. Pat frowned:

"There's reason in plenty, Colonel, but you're jumping off on the wrong foot. I can call myself attached to the Special Branch of the Yard, for the purposes of this affair. Telephone Chief Inspector Trivett, and confirm that statement. If he says 'yes,' I want your word you'll let nothing of this affair pass your lips."

Adams raised his brows.

"You *seem* serious. I'll make the promise, except—well, my wife heard the shot. She'll be curious. I might add," he chuckled: "she's in bed with a feverish cold, and only that and a determined maid would have kept her away."

"For the purposes of this business, you and your wife are considered as one," said Dawlish.

Adams' eyes wrinkled at the corners as he smiled, but he stepped immediately to the telephone. Farningham was regarding his friend sorrowfully. He gaped when Adams finished with the 'phone and said:

"Frankly, I didn't believe it, but Inspector Trivett confirms the statement. He appears anxious to see you, Mr. Dawlish."

"He'll have to wait," said Dawlish, and yawned. "Well now—a *résumé* of this business, friends. I had some reason to believe Miss Farrimond was being threatened, on a kidnap-cum-ransom angle, and it so happened I investigated at the right time. Though what would have happened if you hadn't arrived, Bill, I just don't know. Nor you, sir," he added for Adams's benefit. "It's hush-hush, for Chloë's sake of course."

"Almost plausible," Adams said with a smile, "but it simply means you don't want to talk. Now, unless there's anything else I can do, I'll go. But do, please, call on me for anything." He reached the door, and turned to add: "We've a spare room—if you think Miss Farrimond would be more comfortable there, please say the word."

"It might be useful, thanks a lot," smiled Dawlish. "Oh, there's one thing. Doesn't Miss Farrimond usually have two maids in the flat?"

"Yes, and a cook. Er—" Adams looked embarrassed. "I've heard it said that she sends them out occasionally."

Dawlish grinned. "Nothing doing this time; she was due to go out herself. Poor Chloë!"

"Actually I've a considerable regard for her," said Adams. "And Phyllis—my wife—has too. They're by way of being friends." Adams smiled again, and went out.

Dawlish sprawled in an easy chair and eyed his friend with some amusement. "Well, Bill. Nice of you to come. How long are you here for?"

"Ten days, and let me tell you that a week of it's engaged," said Farningham with spirit. "Diana's coming to town on Saturday, and not you, nor Chloë, nor the whole police force will get me in this kind of shindy once she's here."

"This is a day for faithful swains," Dawlish grinned. Then, more serious, added: "But before we start talking, old man, we've arrangements to make. Chloë'll need nursing, of course."

"Yes, decidedly."

"So we need a nice friendly nursing-home where they won't ask a lot of questions and won't object to a couple of flatfoots in the neighbourhood. Know of one?"

"Sister Em will look after her," said Farningham.

Sister Em, Dawlish knew, ran a small but exclusive nursing-home for the unfortunate ones of Mayfair. She was a large, bouncing woman, as good-natured as she was shrewd, and of the many secrets that entered her head, only those came out that did not matter. Thus she could pose both as a purveyor of information and a holder of confidences, and increase her prosperity. Nothing that was not lawful happened at her nursing-home in Bayswater, where she contrived to keep both her staff and her patients happy—no mean feat.

"Sister Em it is," said Dawlish, "I'd forgotten her. She can send a private ambulance, can't she?"

"Yes, I'll give her a ring." Farningham did so, while Dawlish examined his face in a mirror and grimaced. He was still feeling the effects of the two rounds with Grey & Company, and he was not wholly satisfied. He did not altogether blame himself; the ammonia trick had the merit of effectiveness as well as simplicity, and somehow it seemed typical of Messrs. Grey.

More: he had heard of the silver hair-brushes, but he did not know their importance. He had been assured that if the police had taken the pale-faced man into custody, it would have meant imprisonment for Chloë: for some reason which he could not properly explain, Dawlish did not find that difficult to believe.

One credit item was the wallet and oddments from the pale-faced man's pockets.

Dawlish had them in his coat, and he looked through them again: but they offered little. There was a silver pencil and a gold cigarette case, but neither were monogrammed. Nor was the wallet or the gold Hunter which he had annexed. He opened the back of it, hoping to find something inside that would be worthy of interest, but the jewelled movements were all that met his eye. From the twenty-one pounds in notes of various denominations and the handful of silver and copper there was nothing to be derived.

Which left the envelope addressed to Mr. Wilfrid Askew, at 18 Snow Court, St. John's Wood. At least Mr. Askew might be worth investigating. But that fact served to emphasise the misfortune of Chloë's drugged stupor: there was so much she might have said.

He was waiting to telephone a gymnasium in Aldgate High Street, from which two physically-perfect gentlemen of Cockney breed would gladly come and for a spell watch over Chloë at Sister Em's—he was determined for the time being to keep the essentials of the affair from the Yard, and hoped he could do so until Chloë had recovered. Waiting, he considered the broad outlines of the affair, and marvelled at the good fortune which had made him visit the club, and thus talk with Andy Cunningham. Actually, of course, it was a normal thing; he saw Andy most days when he was in town.

He was aware, if only vaguely, of an uncomfortable feeling that Andy could have known something of what was going to happen. It was unlikely, but many unlikely things had already happened.

Dawlish stopped thinking. Farningham was having some trouble with Sister Em's number and was complaining into the telephone as Dawlish reached the door leading into the front room. And Dawlish uttered a profanity with feeling, making the doctor swing round.

"What—"

"We're a precious couple," growled Dawlish savagely. "We both forgot the man you wounded. He's gone, taking the bullet with him I shouldn't wonder. By jove, that man has pluck!"

CHAPTER VII

MR. ABRAHAM LARRAMY

There were other things remarkable about Mr. Abraham Larramy besides the fact that the five vowels in his name were all 'a'. Although Dawlish did not know his name nor where to find him, he would never forget Larramy's pallid face, or those feverish, brilliant eyes—eyes which seemed a little insane, although the man's actions were certainly sane enough. He had temperament, as those who worked for him knew only too well, and he could be violent. Yet in some things he was reasonable, and he rewarded good service with good wages.

One of the most remarkable things about him was that the police did not suspect his law-defying habits.

Larramy, at fifty-three, had done so many intolerable things that, had his true history been recorded, no one would have believed it. Although he used a gun only in emergency he was a remarkably good shot, and he liked to send his bullet between the eyes, taking what might be called a professional pride in so doing. He had handled dope for longer than he liked to remember, for he was conscious of middle age and like so many men who dispensed death freely, had a horror of it.

He had sent three men, innocent of murder, to the electric chair when he should have been there himself. He had taken part in South American revolutions, supplying the ammunition, and on one dark occasion blowing up a block of tenements and three hundred souls to kill three men who might have betrayed him. He was a man of remarkable achievement, he was completely unmoral, although in his guise as a respectable citizen scrupulously honest, but there was one thing and one thing only for which he had a genuine passion, or even real regard.

He loved music.

So few people had known Larramy for more than three or four years of his life that none could say with certainty that he was not likely to have a soul—although most believed it. Yet that queer kink in the man made him worship at the shrine of music, believed by so many to be the one true expression of the soul. He was no mean pianist, and he had held hundreds enthralled by his violin solos; a man who could make the strings and the instrument speak although without words.

Thus Abraham Larramy.

For four years a man had worked for Larramy who actually liked and was loyal to him. There were reasons. There was something of hero-worship in the attitude of servant to employer, for there was no envy in Bilson: he was prepared to carry out all orders, and to be glad of any word of praise. Knowing the man thoroughly, Larramy gave that praise occasionally yet not too fully: he knew that if he gave Bilson instructions they would be obeyed to the letter, unless the man was dead. On the other hand, he knew also that it was useless to expect Bilson to work on his own initiative at any time.

In a house on the outskirts of Wimbledon Common, a large house fully-staffed with servants and where Larramy was known as Larramy since the name was as good as any other and did not figure on police records, Larramy sat in a study which had been furnished completely by the previous owner of the house, a retired solicitor, and the walls of the study were lined with legal tomes. The furniture was heavy and dark, the curtains were of red plush, the oak panelling was dark. To Larramy it seemed 'class'—and certainly it provided a background of the utmost respectability.

The house had been altered a little—just enough. There were rooms in the roof and others in the cellar where things the police would not approve of happened: but the alterations had been carried out by trustworthy workmen, who would never talk of what they had done.

In every way, thought Larramy, it was what he wanted. There were four exits—two known, being the front and rear, two unknown, one leading from the cellar to the end of the back garden—which garden was of some acre-and-a-half—and the other at the side of the house and leading almost directly on to the Common. It was a large house, with some seventeen rooms. It was quiet and secluded, and yet admirably central for operating in London or the Southern counties. It was only twenty-five minutes from Victoria, for instance, and while Dawlish and Farningham were talking in Chloë's flat, Larramy was sitting at the large, walnut desk in the study, telephone in hand.

A drab voice was speaking.

"It was inevitable, sir, several others joined him, and we had no choice but to leave at once, the business could not be discussed in those circumstances. The woman, I am afraid, was obstinate; most obstinate."

"You left her there?"

"As I intimated, yes," said Lancelot Grey. "I endeavoured to carry out all of your instructions, but—"

"You fell down on the job," snapped Larramy, and he did not sound pleased. "I'll talk to you later, but look after Cunningham, and make it quickly. How long'll Bilson be?"

There was a moment of hesitation, and then Grey said softly:

"He was unfortunately detained, sir."

"What?" Larramy pushed back his chair, and had Dawlish seen him he would have recognised the glittering rage in his eyes. "You left Bilson—Bilson! Get him, I tell you!"

"He met with an accident, sir." Even the drab voice of Lancelot Grey suggested that he was nervous. "Everything possible was done, but—"

"He's—dead?"

"I—"

And then, as Larramy was glaring at the wall, trying to find words, the door of the study opened. Larramy looked up— and he banged the telephone down without another word and sprang to the side of Luke Bilson. For Bilson was almost as pale as his employer, and his lips were twitching with pain. Over his Harris tweeds was a mackintosh covering the blood-soaked jacket, and he sat down abruptly as Larramy reached him.

"In the shoulder, Boss, I ain't hurt bad. Gimme a drink, will you?" He licked his lips, and Larramy hurried to find the whisky. Bilson drank it neat at a gulp, and his eyes watered as he handed the glass back. "Ma Finnigan can dress me up okay, but I reckon I'll be off duty for a week or so."

"That's—all right," said Larramy. He felt oddly relieved, having for the first time realised from the shock Grey had given him, just how much he had come to rely on his bodyguard: "Quite all right, Bilson. We'll soon have you fit. Let me see it."

He pressed a bell three times, and then took off the mackintosh and, with surprisingly gentle hands, cut away the sleeve of Bilson's coat. He was talking all the time, and Bilson made an effort to answer his questions. Bilson was scrupulously honest in his description of the flight from de Mond Mansion.

"I don't know how many—I saw three, Boss. One older'n you. Grey couldn't help it, he did the right thing." Bilson moved his arm and winced, and there was a tap on the door.

"A minute," called Larramy. "Now, Bilson, one more effort. Cunningham was not hurt, nor the others? The woman, for instance?"

"All okay, Boss, only—" He gritted his teeth: he was weak from loss of blood, but he contrived to mutter: "only what's Cunningham's first name?"

"Andrew."

"The other bloke called him something diff'rent. Pat, I think. I—" Bilson gasped suddenly, and then his head drooped backwards. He would do no more talking for a while, and Larramy raised his voice.

"Come in—hurry!"

The door opened, and a woman entered who might have been sixty or eighty. She was in black from head to foot, and shiny black beads drooped over her ample bosom. Her hair was pure white but plentiful, and she wore it piled up on her head. With her majestic figure it should have made her seem stately, but the harridan's face beneath the hair robbed her of that illusion. It was a thin face, with the skin stretched tight across the hooked nose and the high cheek-bones, and her eyes were bright and unwinking, like shiny black berries. Her mouth was thin, little more than an ugly, almost colourless gash, and her pointed chin was pock-marked, as were her cheeks.

She rustled as she walked.

"What is it now?" Her voice was strident.

"Bilson's hurt. Get a bedroom ready for him at once, and tell

Sloane there's a bullet to come out—if you can get Sloane sober. Hot water, and—"

"I don't need tellin'," barked Ma Finnigan, and she went out as abruptly as she had entered. Larramy was too used to her to let that worry him. She ruled the staff at Clunes—the name had not been altered since Larramy had taken over—with an iron hand, as well as some of the residents, for six people lived there besides Larramy. She terrified the maids, none of whom was of unblemished reputation, and her accounts were accurate to a farthing. She snarled at Larramy as fearlessly as at a maid, and yet she was invaluable: nothing ever went wrong inside the house.

She did not go outside.

She lived in terror of the police, and she had not gone beyond the confines of the walled garden for three years. Three times she had served sentences for illegal operations, and the fourth time her 'patient' had died. There had been a murder charge preferred but never taken to court, for Ma had disappeared: she had known Bilson and Bilson had brought her to Abraham Larramy. Larramy let her talk as she liked, only occasionally silencing her—and there was one way of doing that: by talking of the past.

Now he was too concerned about Bilson and what Bilson had told him. 'Andrew Cunningham', that *was* the name. *Andrew*. Why should he be called 'Pat'? Why had he behaved so differently from what they had been led to expect?

As Bilson was carried out on an improvised stretcher by two men in shirt-sleeves, Larramy lifted the telephone and called a Mayfair number. He talked, briefly, to a smooth-voiced man who knew his subject.

"Nearly six feet high," said the smooth voice, "dark, with a long—"

"That's enough!" snapped Larramy.

His eyes were foul as he waited for the exchange to discon-
nect and then put through a call to the St. John's Wood house
where Lancelot Grey was staying. Grey answered, and Larramy
snarled:

"That wasn't Cunningham, you fool, it was someone else. Get
hold of Cunningham right away, understand? Don't fall down
this time—*get* him!"

For the second time he rang off without regard for Lancelot
Grey's feelings—what time Andy Cunningham had finished a
long drawn-out luncheon and was breathing afresh, for he had
told his lovely Betty of the appointment with Chloë, and she had
forgiven him. Or at least laughed at him, for she knew her Andy.

She did not know Lancelot Grey, just then.

CHAPTER VIII

DAWLISH IS MORTIFIED

Dawlish was able to appreciate the physical courage of the missing Bilson, but that did nothing to ease his mortification.

"It can't be helped," said Bill philosophically.

"It could have been helped," retorted Dawlish. "And Chloë apart, it's the loss of the one angle we might have found useful."

"I don't like that 'we'," protested Bill.

"Backing out?" asked Dawlish gently.

Bill grinned. "Not exactly, old man, I'll see you through. But I'm a bit worried about what Di'll think. I mean, she's had a go at this kind of thing before, and—"

"She should be grateful that such things happen, since one gave her you," said Pat severely. "Di'll be all right, leave her to me."

"Thank you, I can manage Diana." Farningham was almost stiff; he could joke about anything in the world except his engagement, on which subject he was as humourless as a half-wit.

"Is Sister Em coming?"

"She'll be here, or the ambulance will, in twenty minutes."

"Quick work. I'll ring the Shop."

The 'Shop' being the gymnasium aforementioned, and also known to Farningham, there was no need for explanation. The manager greeted Dawlish warmly over the telephone and said that he would be delighted to despatch two bodyguards.

"Frankie and Ben," he said. "Will they do?"

"Couldn't be better. Could they be ironed?"

"Blimey!" said the manager downrightly. "Like that, is it? Okay, I'll see to it, Mr. D. Usual insurance and what not?"

"Usual insurance and what not," agreed Dawlish, who made private arrangements for anyone from the Shop who risked life and limb when working for him. But as he replaced the receiver he was thinking less of insurance than 'what not.' It was the word Andy Cunningham had used in conjunction with 'flurried'. Chloë, in fact, had allowed Andy to see—or hear—that she was worried: the pale-faced man believed that he knew enough about her to send her to prison for a long spell.

What had Chloë done?

There were other questions of importance, and the most urgent was the association of the Greys and the others with drugs.

Farningham lit a cigarette, and scowled.

"That reminds me, I haven't had lunch."

"Nor me. We could forage in the larder. At least you can: I want a talk with Andy." He went to the telephone while Bill sought the larder, and telephoned Andy Cunningham's flat. The deep voice of Andy's general factotum assured him that Mr. Cunningham was not yet back from lunch.

"Ask him to go to my flat immediately he returns," Dawlish said. "Immediately, Simm: it's important."

"I will see to it, sir."

Dawlish rang the Regal immediately afterwards: Andy and

his Betty had left five minutes before. Beyond leaving word at the club; the only other likely port of call, there was nothing Dawlish could do to trace his friend, except—

Call in Trivett.

Dawlish hesitated, scratching his chin, as Bill came from the kitchen with a tray of bread, butter, cheese and ham.

"Best I can do," said Bill gloomily. "What are you looking thoughtful about?"

"Just thoughts," said Dawlish. "Cut some bread, William. I've another call to make."

Farningham cut bread with an unpractised hand, while Dawlish telephoned Whitehall 1212. He was keenly aware of the possibility of his real identity becoming known to the Greys, and once that happened Andy himself was in danger; it was a chance that must not be taken, and he was wondering whether he should have acted earlier. In every way, he admitted to Bill as he waited for Trivett, he had reason to curse himself.

"Why?" asked Trivett at the other end of the line.

"Trying to interfere in other folks' love affairs," said Dawlish blandly. "Triv, I'd particularly like a talk with a Mr. Andrew Cunningham, of Broom Street, W.1. A friend of mine, and he's out with his lady. Can you get him for me?"

"Why?" asked Trivett again.

"I'm not yet sure," said Dawlish, and dropped his bantering tone. "But it's serious, Trivett. Andy should be within three miles of the Regal, and he's running a Mercedes. Can do?"

"All right." Trivett sounded reluctant, and Dawlish grinned to himself. "If you'll put that call out, I'll give you one or two more questions," he offered.

"Hold on," said Trivett.

Dawlish accepted a hunk of bread and cheese from Farningham, and waited for the Inspector's 'carry on'.

"Two gentlemen, reputed brothers, named Grey and looking grey," he said when it came.

"They don't call anything to mind," said Trivett after a pause.

"Hmm. What about Bilson? A clear roughneck type—with some American experience, I shouldn't wonder."

"It probably isn't his real name," said Trivett. "If you can give me a detailed description, or finger-prints—"

"Finger-prints, maybe," said Dawlish. And again he was appalled by his own carelessness. "Triv, there's been a spot of bother at the flat of a friend of mine, not unconnected with this business—or I think not. I've got to hold a watching brief for the time being, but if you'll send a man over for finger-prints it might prove useful."

"But—" began Trivett.

"My game, my rules," Dawlish reminded him.

"Don't carry that too far," retorted Trivett. "What's the address?"

Dawlish gave it, and: "Even a policeman will know that's Chloë Farrimond's flat, but Chloë's not here and doesn't know a thing about it. Strictly hush-hush, Triv, or you'll break a sequence we might find useful. All right?"

"All right," said Trivett, reluctantly. Then hung up and rang the finger-print department.

A man was sent over immediately but missed Chloë, who had been taken to Sister Em's ten minutes before he arrived. Trivett, meanwhile, asked for and was granted an interview with Sir Archibald Morely.

Morely was not yet forty, young for his job but none the less efficient for that. A strict disciplinarian, his rigid justness made him popular at the Yard. He took his job seriously, admitted that he would never make an active C.I.D. man, yet possessed a quick organising ability which made him invaluable. He held the strings of the C.I.D. unobtrusively but effectively.

Tall, lean, dark, not handsome and yet distinguished, with thinning black hair brushed straight back from a high forehead and disconcertingly frank grey eyes, his sensitive lips curved in amusement when he saw Trivett's expression.

"Sit down, Trivett. Is Dawlish worrying you?"

Trivett smiled. "Sorry I gave myself away like that, sir."

"I've seen the same expression before when he's been active," said Morely dryly. "Awkward customer, Dawlish. It's impossible to be sure just what he's doing and thinking. But we can rely on him to mean well."

"He scares me at times," admitted Trivett. "He takes so much in his own hands, and we've rather asked for it this time. He tells me—"

Morely listened without interruption, frowning a little when Trivett finished.

"Yes. . . . It doesn't seem possible that he's been working so quickly, but with Dawlish it could be."

"Things come to meet him," said Trivett with feeling. "We spent a month looking for something, and it looks as if he's walked right into it. The thing that worries me, sir, is that Chloë Farrimond had been at the Black Out Club every night for a month or more. She's always with Sir Louis Morrell."

Morely frowned. "Morrell? Not too savoury, Trivett."

"No, sir. If one wanted to imagine a man who could be handling the dope, Morrell fits."

"I know," said Morely. "He skates on very thin ice, but we can't be sure that he's overstepped the mark. However, it is a point. Does Dawlish know of his association with Miss Farrimond?"

"If he doesn't, he soon will."

"Leave things as they are for the time being," Morely decided finally, "Dawlish will tell us when there's anything to work on.

We *need* quick results, and he just might get them for us. We may have to wink a lot, but you understand that."

"Perfectly, sir," said Trivett.

But he was troubled. And more troubled when, two hours afterwards, he learned that one set of prints found in several places at Chloë Farrimond's flat belonged to a man who had seen the inside of Dartmoor and Parkhurst. The photograph of the man Dawlish would have recognized as Bilson was sufficient to tell him that Bilson (then known as Grayson) was the type who might be expected to have a record of robbery with violence. The lowering brows, close and deep-set eyes, and the loose mouth with the prominent teeth, suggested the *apache* type. There was a note on the dossier which said:

Dangerous when in a corner. Known at times to use a gun. Believed entered U.S.A. during the spring of 1954. Not heard of since.

Morely and Trivett compared notes over this discovery, but could reach no conclusion beyond the obvious one that Dawlish might indeed be getting results.

"There's one other thing, sir," said Trivett. "He wanted to talk with a Mr. Andrew Cunningham, who was given that message at half-past three, when he was seen in Putney with a friend. A lady friend. Should Cunningham be watched?"

"No—leave it to Dawlish."

"Very good, sir," said Trivett, and went out.

Meanwhile, Pat Dawlish, Bill Farningham and Andy Cunningham were in Dawlish's flat. Cunningham had exuded melancholy disapproval as he entered.

"You're a friend," he was saying. "You pretend to get me clear of one thing, and then send a police message out for me! Betty'll think I'm a consort of crooks before you've finished. None of your funny business, Pat. Betty's waiting downstairs and it's cold. What's the bother? How's Chloë?"

"Sleeping after the shock," said Dawlish amiably. "Andy, how worried did she seem on the phone?"

"We-ell—she *pleaded* for a talk," said Cunningham, frowning and looking puzzled. "Last thing she'd normally do. As a matter of fact it's okay with Betty, so I'm seeing Chloë tonight for an hour."

"I don't think so," said Dawlish. He gave up the idea—temporarily—that Andy could conceivably know anything about the Greys. "Did she give you a parting present at the end of the engagement?"

"She did, yes." Cunningham stared, and then his eyes widened. "I say, Pat, what have you been doing to your face?"

"Never mind my face. What was the present?"

"A pair of silver-backed brushes."

"Which aren't at your flat."

Cunningham's lips opened. "How the devil did you know that?"

"A little bird whispered to me," said Dawlish cheerfully. "Andy, you are in deep waters—take it from me. Was there any special significance in that choice of gift—any special circumstances of place or timing?"

Cunningham stared at him.

"Pat *are* you quite batty? What the deuce do those brushes matter? Where's Chloë, and what's she been saying?"

"Special significance or circumstances," repeated Dawlish firmly.

"Of course there weren't. I was a bit surprised—a pair of gloves would have been more the thing."

"What happened to the brushes?"

Andy looked embarrassed.

"Well—I've about six pairs, you know. Not a great deal of use to me, and I sent 'em to a Sale of Oddments for some Appeal or other. Between you and me," said Andy hastily, to excuse himself, "after Betty had said the word, I cleared out everything I'd ever had from the others. It seemed the thing to do, you know—and pushed 'em all off to this sale. About a week ago, or a day or two longer."

"Who was organising it?" snapped Dawlish, and Cunningham was startled by the expression in his eyes.

"Lady Milhampton. She—"

"When was the sale?"

"Yesterday, I think."

"There's just a chance they've not been sold," said Dawlish, and reached for the telephone. "Andy, we've got to have a sober talk—Betty can't freeze downstairs any longer. Slip down for her; the next room's comfortable. Switch the fire on in there, Bill . . . hallo? Lady Milhampton, please."

"Very good, sir." Dawlish was known at the Milhampton *ménage*. Lady Milhampton had a son with whom Dawlish had played much cricket.

"*Patrick!*" Lady Milhampton did not exactly gush, but she created the impression of deep enthusiasm. "I was speaking of you, only yesterday—"

"I'm afraid this is rather urgent," Dawlish apologised, cutting her short. "But I wonder—Andy Cunningham sent some silver brushes to the sale. Could they be available still?"

"Brushes—Andy? Oh, I remember! I'm afraid not, Patrick, someone bought them, I don't quite know who—oh, but I do! It was Sir Louis Morrell. I remember he bought several things and paid quite handsomely for them. He—"

"*Dawlish!*"

The voice from the door blasted across Dawlish's ears so

sharply and with such emphasis that he jerked his head from the instrument to see Cunningham standing there with a queer, strained expression on his face.

"I'll ring again, Lady Milhampton, thanks a lot."

He rang off abruptly: he could apologise gracefully later.

"What's the trouble, Andy?" he urged.

"Betty's gone."

"Gone?"

"I—I can't make it out," said Cunningham tensely. "The car's not there, but I know she couldn't drive it. There was a torn handkerchief on the pavement, one of hers. What were you talking about just now?"

Dawlish snapped: "Wait a minute," and dialled Whitehall 1212. "Inspector Trivett—all right, Sergeant Munk will do . . . Munk, put out a call for Mr. Cunningham's Mercedes again, at once and it's urgent. The driver might be awkward . . . don't argue, do it!"

He replaced the receiver, and his face was gaunt as he eyed Andy—while Cunningham looked like a ghost.

CHAPTER IX

QUEST FOR BETTY

"Sorry," said Dawlish stiffly. "Andy, there's no time for a lot of talk at the moment. You and those brushes are wanted badly by gentlemen who won't stand on ceremony. They're more anxious about the brushes than you, and they've an idea you're hiding them deliberately. Betty could—I say could—have been taken for a ride to put the wind up you."

The telephone rang.

Dawlish turned towards it, and Farningham crossed to the sideboard to fix the drink Cunningham clearly needed. But the soda was still squirting in when Dawlish said harshly:

"Yes, speaking."

The tone of his voice held the others tense—but could he have heard the flat voice of Mr. Lancelot Grey, Cunningham would have been far more perturbed.

"Oh, Mr. Dawlish—" if it were possible for Grey to chuckle, he did so then. "I understand that a strange mistake was made. So foolish of you to run yourself into trouble for other people. I have been very busy since I left you, and—Mr. Cunningham *is* fond of his *fiancée*, isn't he?"

Dawlish took a grip on himself.

"Meaning what?"

"She looked so cold, my brother has taken her for a ride, to where she'll get warmer. We can move very fast, you see. I hope Cunningham can, too. We are quite prepared to exchange the brushes for the hostage—but it must be quickly."

"Cunningham hasn't got them."

"You can hardly expect me to believe that," said Mr. Grey urbanely. "You bluffed magnificently before, but I want you to understand you cannot do it again—not successfully, that is. Oh, Dawlish—we are serious, you know. Miss Carruthers is a charming girl, most charming. And not, I believe, in the habit of taking—er—stimulants. Such a pity if she began now, wouldn't it?"

Dawlish felt stiff and cold.

"Grey, if—"

"The brushes," said Grey gently. "Otherwise I'm afraid she will learn the delights of cocaine. Or perhaps opium. I am serious, Dawlish. I will call for the brushes in three hours: three hours precisely, at seven o'clock. Be *quite* certain to have them."

And the telephone went dead.

Dawlish replaced it with an effort, and looked at Cunningham sombrely.

"Sorry, old man: the theory fitted. She'll be all right—but they want the brushes in exchange."

"I haven't got them!" Cunningham's eyes were wild, his breathing unsteady. "For God's sake, man—"

"I know where they are," Dawlish said. "I'll try to get them. Listen—" He repeated the gist of Grey's words, but omitted the reference to drugs, and as he spoke he realised that Cunningham was under the strain of great emotion; that to him, the girl meant everything. He seemed to see a new Cunningham, a man who was lost without his beloved, and who was terribly afraid.

But why not fighting mad? He could have been expected to be, after the first shock.

The query registered itself at the back of Dawlish's mind.

"You and Bill," he said, "will stay here. If I'm not back when Grey arrives, tell him I've gone to try to find them. Tell him what happened to them but *don't* give him Lady Milhampton's name. There've been a dozen different sales and it might be any one of them."

Cunningham sat down heavily in a chair.

"I suppose you know what you're doing. But—Pat, if anything happens to that girl—"

"Easy, I said." Dawlish smiled and rested a hand on Andy's shoulder. "This is only a preliminary skirmish—Betty's an aside that doesn't matter to them. Leave things to Uncle Pat, and don't move from here, either of you, until I'm back. Or I've 'phoned. Watch things, Bill."

"Right," said Farningham, more emphatically than he felt. The essential thing, he realised, was to keep Cunningham in some degree easy of mind, but that was going to be hard.

The telephone rang again.

"*Blast* it," said Dawlish, and picked up the receiver. "Hallo . . . oh, yes Munk . . . right, thanks a lot." He hung up and grinned crookedly at the others. "Our Mr. Grey is careful. The Benz has been stranded in Chelsea; Betty's changed cars."

"Damn it—shouldn't the police be looking for her? Shouldn't—"

"No," said Dawlish decisively, "we don't want her found by the police if we can do it ourselves. I'll be back."

He went out quickly, and hurried downstairs. The first and obvious thing to do was to get the brushes back from Morrell, but already something was worrying him. For Morrell and Chloë were reputed to be good friends; their frequent appearances together at the Black Out clinched that fact. Perhaps more than friends—Chloë's reputation would stand it. So:

Had Morrell bought those brushes by accident?

Or because he knew Chloë had given them to Cunningham?

It was impossible to be sure. Dawlish pushed the thought aside as he hailed a passing taxi and gave the address of Morrell, who had one of the three remaining private houses in Park Lane and kept it in considerable state. His footmen were flunkeys and dressed like it; he maintained a household reminiscent of the Regency days, and there was some justification for his claim to be the modern Beau Brummel.

As the cab turned into Piccadilly, Dawlish had a moment's disquiet about Cunningham: the youngster was not acting as he had expected. In fact it was the first time for years that Dawlish had thought of him as a youngster. His *blasé* air, his sophistication, and his playboy attitude had been wiped away as if they had never existed.

Had he been *surprised*?

He didn't seem so, Dawlish admitted, and then looked out of the small rear window of the cab. He was not surprised to see an Austin quite close to him: nor that the driver was the younger Grey; he had expected a shadow.

He opened the glass partition and changed his directions.

"Make it the Cumberland, please."

"Right, sir."

He stepped out, paid the cabby, and entered the Cumberland. He did not stay long, for he saw a passenger from Grey's car going to the side entrance, which was precisely what he had expected. He went into Oxford Street again, and Grey was approaching the *foyer*, moving back in surprise when he saw Dawlish.

Dawlish approached him without hesitation.

"Surprised, little man? Not as much as you're going to be."

He was very close to Jonathan Grey—so close that it seemed impossible that he could deliver a right-arm jab to the *solar plexus* with such force. But he did, and Grey gasped with the sudden pain and doubled up. A dozen people looked round in surprise, including a policeman twenty yards away.

Dawlish moved fast.

While Grey was still holding his stomach, Dawlish had slipped into the Corner House, where he was easily lost in the crowd. He made his way quickly but unostentatiously to the other entrance, went out, found a taxi, and gave Morrell's address for the second time.

In three minutes, he was outside the grey stone porch of Morrell's house. He had only one thing in his mind—the importance of getting the brushes quickly. He could not even think clearly of their mystery, of what possible secret they could hold. Nor, for that matter, how Chloë had come to have them.

Obviously she would *buy* the brushes from somewhere.

Dawlish frowned as an idea flashed through his mind. But it went immediately the door opened. The footman on the threshold wore knee breeches, beige stockings, a beige coat and a supercilious expression.

Dawlish handed him his card.

"The matter is urgent," he said. "Please tell Sir Louis at once."

"Sir Louis," said the footman expressionlessly, "is not at home, sir. He is out of town."

The sharp shock of that statement left Dawlish for a moment too disappointed for words. He knew that Morrell had been in London for most of the week: he had not dreamed there might be difficulty in finding him.

"You're sure?" he said; and knew that he had invited the disdainful gleam in the footman's eyes.

"*Quite* sure, sir."

"Where can I find him?"

"I am not at liberty to discuss the matter, sir."

Dawlish felt violent, but recovered himself. He smiled, and the footman visibly thawed.

"All right, I'll see his secretary. I must get in touch with Sir Louis immediately. Send my card in at once, will you?"

"His secretary, sir, is at the Staines house. You may be more fortunate there, sir."

"Staines?" said Dawlish, and then remembered that Morrell had a large house on the river at Staines—a house which many people believed to be the reverse of respectable. "Oh, yes, of course."

Smiling his thanks, he hurried into the street. He was forced to walk for several minutes before finding a cab and giving the address of his garage, in a mews quite near his flat. Ten minutes later, he was at the wheel of a gleaming Allard.

The going was slow along Piccadilly, but he had a fairly free run up through Hyde Park, and hummed more quickly than the law allowed along Bayswater Road. He was approaching Shepherd's Bush when he realised for the first time that he was followed: Jonathan Grey, in the Austin, was still on his tail.

And as he faced that fact, he wondered whether he *had* been seen at Morrell's.

CHAPTER X

GUNFIRE

He had not.

Grey had recovered from the blow, pretended that he was subject to stomach cramp, and stepped into a telephone box. He had called the Wimbledon house—and in the interval, Abraham Larramy had been learning things of Pat Dawlish.

"Find him again," Larramy snapped, "and don't make *any* mistake: put him clean away. Who've you got with you?"

"Kramm."

"He'll do, he's got everything he wants in the car. Never mind the risk, get it done. Understand that?"

"Ye-es," said Jonathan Grey.

He was not as mild a man as he looked, but there were some things that worried him—chief of these being the possibility of being caught. On the other hand, he had worked for Larramy long enough to know that the big man would not give decisive orders unless they were essential. The order was to kill Dawlish and to make no mistakes: and Kramm, a one-time American mobsman, had a Thomson sub-machine-gun in a case beneath the rear seat of the Austin.

The kiosk was near the entrance Kramm was optimistically covering. A short, thick-set man with a blue jowl and bold, brown eyes, he shook his head as Grey came up.

"Not a thing."

"He's about somewhere—we'll go back to his flat," Grey said, and did not explain how he had 'lost' Dawlish. "And hurry. You've got your tools?"

Kramm's eyes widened.

"Like that, huh?"

"But not in London." Grey shivered. "I hope not, anyway."

He did not speak again until, turning into Brook Street, he saw Dawlish at the wheel of an Allard. Grey drove well, and kept out of sight until they neared Shepherd's Bush. He knew then that he had been noticed, but he doubted that Dawlish would suspect what was coming to him.

Grey felt his heart beating fast.

Kramm, in the rear, had unlocked the case and was fitting the tommy-gun together. By the time they had reached Hammersmith he could report himself ready, but Grey shook his head. Chiswick—the Great West Road—

There was surprisingly little traffic about, once they were past the factories along that wide ribbon leading to the West, and Grey turned his head, nodding slightly. His eyes were narrowed and he felt cold, but Kramm was as calm as if this were a New York back street. He hoisted the gun to his knees, while Grey trod more heavily on the accelerator. The Austin leapt forward, developing far greater engine-power than it should have done, and Dawlish saw that within ten seconds the distance between him and the pursuer was lessened by half to fifty yards.

Forty—

He went right out, and the needle of the Allard quivered towards the ninety mark and past it. Ninety-two—three—four—

The Austin was checked, but after a few seconds gradually gained, continued to gain—was no more than twenty yards behind.

Why?

If he wanted to follow, he would have been more discreet. Why should he try to pass at the first deserted stretch?

Dawlish sensed the reason.

He was armed, but he doubted whether he could handle the two men in the Austin, suspected what kind of attack was likely to come. Nothing about the Greys would surprise him; he was prepared for ruthlessness on a large scale. And he believed he was going to be shot at as they passed.

If they passed.

Fifteen yards—

He saw the sun glinting on something held in the hands of the passenger in the Austin, and it did not look like an automatic. Dawlish acted then, knowing he had to take a desperate chance or go under.

He swung his wheel to the right.

The front wheels of the Allard hit the central verge, went over, skidded, and met the surface of the London-bound carriageway. The rear wheels lifted entirely, the car slithered and was out of control—

While the Austin flashed by.

Dawlish saw the streaks of flame coming from the Tommy-gun but the roaring of his own engine drowned the *tap-tap-tap-tap* that he knew was coming. It drowned the sound of the bullets rattling against the wings of the Allard and biting their way through. He saw three small holes leap into the windscreen in front of him, while the car slithered across the road, and a driver coming towards him hooted stridently in warning.

For a moment Dawlish thought a crash was inevitable.

The other car swerved towards the pavement, its tyres screaming and Dawlish caught a glimpse of the scared driver. The shooting had stopped, for the Austin was fifty yards away and still travelling fast. Dawlish could do nothing, just waited. The Allard reared over to one side, quivered—and then came down on all four wheels.

Dawlish felt the relief of that escape as the driver from the other car opened his door and leapt towards him.

"Are you all right? Good Heaven, I saw—"

"Shooting, I know," said Dawlish, and grinned wryly. "Police—that is, I'm police—and they didn't like me. I wonder if this bus still goes?"

The engine had stalled, but it started smoothly. He swung round, in front of the startled eyes of the other motorist, crossed the verge again and drove towards Staines. The Austin was out of sight. . . .

He left the Allard in the station car park and took a taxi to Morrell's place. He sat well back, watching the road ahead but he did not see the Austin, and that puzzled him. It might have doubled back and tried to pick up his trail, but the most likely places for it to try after failing on the Great West Road were Staines and Slough—with Staines the more likely.

Grey, apparently, had not thought so.

They crossed the river bridge and took the sharp left turn on to the Chertsey Road, which Dawlish knew reasonably well. Once off the main road, however, he was at a loss, and was glad he had hired the cab: it would have taken him precious minutes to locate Morrell, himself.

A high hedge of yew appeared on the left side of a narrow country lane; then the gates of River Lodge, Morrell's so well-known establishment. The cabby swung through on to the drive and pulled up outside the front portals of a small yet imposing house, some thirty years old. It was no more than a week-end river haunt for Morrell, but the extensive gardens were in superb condition; the lawns smiling beneath the late afternoon sun, wallflowers already gay, tulips and late daffodils nodding in the light wind.

From the drive Dawlish could see the river, flowing gently past. On the far side there were trees, with an occasional willow drooping its long arms into the water. A swan floated majestically by; gulls circled over one of the lawns.

A spot to love, thought Dawlish—he was capable of odd sentiments even at times of stress—and one worthy of an owner more likely to appreciate it than the present one.

Morrell lived on less ceremony here, and a pretty maid opened the door. So pretty, that Dawlish smiled widely as he handed in his card and was ushered into a small but charmingly furnished lounge. A lounge, he would have said, that spoke of a woman's hand, although Morrell was a bachelor.

The door had been closed, but he opened it an inch or two before he lighted a cigarette. The window looked on to lawns and the river, the peacefulness of the scene came to him even more vividly.

But not for long.

It was broken, even blasted, by a scream that came from somewhere above him. A woman's scream, and one of terror, piercing through Dawlish as he swung round towards the door.

And it came again.

CHAPTER XI

MURDER MOST FOUL

Dawlish reached the hall at the same time as a startled manser-vant who came from the domestic quarters. What the man thought at the sight of the stranger did not trouble Dawlish, who reached the stairs first and rushed up them. The cry had not been repeated a second time, but there was the sound of a girl gasping or sobbing, as though for breath. And then, as he reached the spacious landing—remarkable, like the hall, for the comparative lack of furniture—he heard a man's voice.

"What is it, girl? What is it?"

Despite the urgency of the words and the note of anxiety in them, the voice was smooth and oily. Although he had never heard Morrell from close at hand, Dawlish knew it was Morrell speaking. He was standing in a wide passage from which several doors opened—and crouching against the wall, gasping for breath, was the maid who had admitted Dawlish.

She was beside herself, and there would be no sensible answer from her. But Morrell kept shaking her shoulder, and his voice repeated the question over and over again.

"What is it, girl? What is it?"

Dawlish had an impression of a big man, dressed in black; of dark crinkly hair, and a face so handsome that it seemed too good to be true. Then he reached the couple and snapped:

"Supposing you look and see?"

He waited for no permission but stepped into the room nearest the girl—and stopped on the threshold, his stomach turning. Small wonder the girl had screamed like that. He felt queasy himself, and had to force himself to step farther in, for the floor and one wall were a mass of blood—blood that had come from the man lying crumpled on the beige carpet. The man lay in so odd a position that his face, with the cut throat, was turned upwards: and the cut gaped.

There was a stiff breeze coming in from the open window, and the curtains fluttered. Automatically, and averting his eyes from the body, Dawlish stepped towards the window. He saw the hooks of a rope ladder on the sill and, looking out, saw the ladder swaying against the wall. Also on the sill were patches of blood, as though the murderer had some on his knees and had left traces when he had climbed from the room.

Dawlish heard a slow: "Oh, my God!"

He turned to see Morrell standing in the doorway, one hand clutching his throat, and the other held in front of him as though to ward off the sight of the thing on the floor. Morrell's face, tanned by three months at Monte Carlo, had lost most of its colour, and was a dirty yellowish shade. His bold eyes were staring, and his fleshy, sensuous mouth was working.

"Pull yourself together," Dawlish snapped, and in that moment he had forgotten his quest for the silver hair-brushes.

"Who is this, Morrell?"

Morrell seemed unaware that he was looking at a total stranger.

"It's—Jeffery."

"Who's Jeffery?"

"My—secretary. Twenty minutes ago I—no, no, it's too horrible, I could never stand the sight of blood! I—"

Dawlish thought the man would swoon, but Morrell suddenly turned and went out. Dawlish followed, to find the maid quieter now, with two others as well as the manservant huddled about her. Not one of them was capable of meeting the emergency, and Morrell himself was likely to be useless. Dawlish said quietly:

"Get the girl to her bedroom, give her a little whisky, and put a hot-water bottle at her feet. See that she isn't left alone." He eyed the manservant. "Who is your doctor?"

"We—we haven't one here." A good-looking youth with crisp, curly hair, he was visibly trembling.

"Find the nearest, and get him here quickly," said Dawlish.

"Very good, sir." The voice of authority was as good as an introduction, and the man turned away quickly while the girls half-carried the sobbing maid along the passage. Morrell was leaning against the wall, and Dawlish's voice was strangely gentle, although the sight of a man knocked to pieces in that way would ordinarily have made him contemptuous.

"All right, Morrell—you'll be all right. You'll need a drink."

"My—room." Morrell's voice was scarcely audible. "Over—there." He pointed to the door opposite that where the man was lying dead, and Dawlish opened it.

It went through his mind that Morrell had come out to see why the maid had screamed, but had thought to pull his door behind him. That might or might not be instructive.

The first room had been a study, barely furnished on strictly modern lines. The same decorative and furnishing scheme was in the bedroom Dawlish entered. It had a singular austerity for a man so reputedly flamboyant in all things.

Morrell sat heavily in an upholstered tubular steel chair.

"It's—ghastly. Ghastly!"

Dawlish saw a cabinet likely to hold whisky, pulled out a decanter and two glasses, and did not trouble to look for soda. Morrell gulped the drink down, while Dawlish's eyes fell on the dressing-table, and he saw the beige-coloured enamel of the hair-brushes.

He remembered the purpose of his visit, and even found a smile: for the next few minutes it was likely to seem almost insignificant. He knew that Trivett believed him to have a nose for trouble, but this was pitching into crime too hurriedly.

He surveyed Morrell, who had regained a tinge of colour: his cheeks were still haggard, and his lips still trembled. In his black eyes, normally so bold and confident, there seemed to be appeal. Then suddenly he stood up, went to a wall-safe hidden by an etching, and opened it with trembling fingers. He drew out a small box, lifted the lid, took a pinch of a powder inside, and sniffed—as an Edwardian would have sniffed at snuff.

The powder was white.

Dawlish's eyes hardened, although he was prepared to admit that a confirmed cocaine-taker would need the drug after that ordeal. It explained the completeness of Morrell's collapse, and made him almost sorry for the man.

Morrell turned, half-defiantly.

"I had to have that—"

"Sit down for a minute," Dawlish said, "and you'll feel better. You won't know me, of course—my name's Dawlish."

"Oh?" said Morrell, without apparent interest. He was staring fixedly at the closed door and seemed hardly to be breathing. But his colour was getting better.

"Dawlish," repeated Pat. "Of Brook Street."

"Oh," said Morrell, and turned his head slowly. As slowly, he sat down, and crossed his legs. "I am glad to meet you, Mr. Dawlish."

The trite words would have been ludicrous but for Dawlish's knowledge that the man was feeling the effect of the drug, and would act oddly for some minutes. He went on:

"I ought to apologize for breaking in so abruptly. But I had called to see you, and the scream rather disturbed me. Morrell, I hesitate to take anything into my own hands—but the police must know about this immediately."

Morrell stared.

"The police? About—oh, Jeffery. Of course. I wonder if you would be good enough to telephone them? Of course they'll have to know, but *Jeffery*! Why on earth has a thing like this happened?" His voice was taking on a deeper note, a confident one: to some people it would have sounded attractive. "It is incredible—and such a ghastly death. Poor Jeffery! Why on earth—!"

It was the first time he had suggested sympathy for his late secretary, and it proved with the other things that he was regaining his usual composure. His eyes had lost the blankness, and heavy lids drooped over them.

"The police will find that out," said Dawlish. "I'll call them now." He reached for the telephone on a bedside table and called the Staines Headquarters, gave brief particulars, and was assured that someone would be sent out immediately. Finished, he looked back at Morrell, who had risen to his feet and was running a well-shaped thumb over his pointed chin.

He was handsome, now.

One might have said magnificent; his black clothes, immaculately cut, fitted his large, fleshy body to perfection. His fine, high forehead, his large black eyes and the delicate lines of his nose helped to make him seem more like a work of art than a man of flesh and blood. Now that he had recovered and the cocaine was working well, he had a strange motionlessness;

and as he stared one eyelid drooped a little lower than the other.

"You were most efficient with that call, Mr. Dawlish—you gave just the right information. May I know why you called to see me?"

"In a moment," said Dawlish. "Had you any idea that this was coming to Jeffery?"

"Any idea? My dear Mr. Dawlish, that is a remarkable suggestion! I trust it was without conscious innuendo." Morrell was suddenly suave and smiling—and, Dawlish instinctively felt, dangerous.

Dangerous—

It was Sir Louis Morrell's reputation that he always played with fire. Company promoter, director of a dozen important industrial combines, racehorse owner, theatre owner, a modern Beau Brummel and Don Juan, a wit—a man of careless millions, poised, self-confident, capable, with the *entrée* to any house and most families—and yet, not quite *de rigueur*. His father and grandfather before him had set the foundation stones of Morrell's prosperity in Morrell & Son, iron-founders. He was sought after by mothers and daughters; he was polite and courteous, even chivalrous, and yet—

Not *quite.*

A man not to be wholly trusted, a man to be a little feared. In short, thought Dawlish, a man recognised to be a dangerous member of the community.

He wondered what the police thought of him.

"No-o," said Dawlish gently, "there was no innuendo intended, Morrell. It seemed the obvious question. After all a murder would not be committed for nothing."

"No," said Morrell suavely. "And I cannot imagine that Jeffery carried anything of importance in his pockets—" He spoke of the dead man casually and almost off-handedly, with a coldness that suggested an utter lack of feeling. "However, the police will doubtless ask me the necessary and *proper* questions, Mr. Dawlish." He smiled slowly. "Perhaps we can now discuss the purpose of your visit. Although before that, I must express my gratitude at your presence of mind and—he glanced towards the safe—"my confidence in your discretion."

Dawlish shrugged.

"Hardly my business, Morrell; some people get drunk, others—well, we needn't go into that. I've come on rather an odd mission. A friend of mine sent some oddments to Lady Milhampton's sale—you'll recall it—by mistake and wishes he had not; a set of silver brushes which were of considerable sentimental value to him. He made inquiries, and learned that you had bought them."

Morrell stared at him, with that odd trick of lowering one eyelid more than the other.

"I see." His voice was silky. "An understandable mistake, Mr. Dawlish. But tell me why Mr. Cunningham considers it necessary to submit such an inquiry through a third party. And tell me also why he should make so grossly careless a *mistake*—" the 'mistake' was sneered—"over a matter of such sentimental value. That is," added Morrell, "tell me if you can."

And Dawlish, meeting that cynical stare evenly, knew that he would not be likely to get the brushes back.

CHAPTER XII

LADY BETTY

At least, thought Dawlish, he must try.

"I'm glad you've been so blunt, Morrell. It makes things much easier. You know who gave him the brushes, of course."

"Of course." Morrell inclined his head. "Why else should I buy them?"

"Hardly my question to answer," smiled Dawlish. "But you will more readily understand that Andy Cunningham doesn't feel it's quite the thing to chase round after them himself. Or hadn't you heard of his latest adventure?"

"He is engaged to Lady Betty Lorne, yes."

"Who might not approve of his past *affaires*," said Dawlish, "but might consider it unfeeling to send sentimental gifts to a rummage sale—glorified or not. Andy's worried."

"If he wants to get the brushes back," said Morrell sharply, "he can come for them himself. Not—" he recovered and his voice softened, grew slower, "not that I would part with them; my interest in Miss Farrimond is considerable, as you doubtless know. Such charming brushes. I always carry them with me," he added suavely. "That is, I intend to, and I believe they are packed with my case in this room."

"I see. Morrell, those brushes can't have cost you more than thirty pounds. I'll buy them for fifty."

"Oh, no, my friend! They are not for sale."

"I hope," said Dawlish, "that you will change your mind."

"But why?"

"Miss Farrimond would doubtless wish you to," said Dawlish.

He saw the change in the other's expression, the quick frown and the sharp intake of breath.

"What do you mean?"

"I am forced to speak in riddles, unfortunately."

"Why aren't you *quite* frank?" demanded Morrell. "At the sale I saw several other things of Mr. Cunningham's, all of equally sentimental value. I am hardly deceived by your foolish story—or are you trying to find the buyers of every relic of Mr. Cunningham's amorous past?"

Dawlish felt his hands itching.

"Every one that matters," he said with forced lightness. "If I remind you that you have already asked me to be discreet, will that help you to change your mind?"

"No," said Morrell, "it will not. After all, you can hardly make capital out of such a minor incident. In fact it would not be wise for you to do so, Mr. Dawlish. And now—" he stood up and stepped towards the door. "Much though I dislike it, I must remind you that the police will shortly be here, and I shall be busy with them. If Mr. Cunningham cares to visit me, I would be happy to talk with him. There are several things that I could say with advantage to that young man. A drink before you go?"

"Thanks, no—I've been drinking at the wrong times all day. And I'm not going just yet, Morrell."

"You're—what?" Morrell's lips tightened.

"And don't suggest throwing me out," said Dawlish pleasantly. "For the time being, I have been co-opted by the police to assist them in a little matter that is worrying them somewhat—a quest for some stolen stuff, Morrell. I've fiddled about on similar things before, as you doubtless know."

"How does that concern—Jeffery?"

"It doesn't. It merely gives me right of entry," beamed Dawlish, and he seemed thoroughly satisfied with himself. "It's always interesting to hear questions and even help with them." He grinned again as he looked at Morrell, but his eyes were not smiling. "For instance, why did you have such a shock when the girl screamed? Why did you keep asking what it was, instead of going to see? Were you a little *afraid* of what might have happened, Morrell?"

Morrell's eyelids drooped.

"I see. . . . Will you be staying if you have the brushes?"

"No, there's no real need—and after all, I'm not engaged on *that* particular job." Dawlish was feeling satisfied with the result of that effort, with the idea which had come swiftly and which—he believed—was well worth the disclosure to Morrell that he was working with the police. "After all, in the circumstances, probably anyone would have been startled."

"You can have the brushes," said Morrell roughly. Crossing to the side of the bed, he picked up a pigskin suitcase. As he opened it, Dawlish noticed his deliberate, careful movements; here was a man who would never be careless, a man instinctively methodical.

He saw Morrell start.

He was quite convinced that the start was genuine, as well as the stupefaction in the black eyes.

"They—they're not *here*! They're gone!"

The transition from exhilaration to depression came swiftly to Dawlish. He crossed to the bed and saw Morrell lift everything out of the case. There were no brushes.

"When was this packed?" Dawlish asked tensely.

"This—this morning, some time. It's incredible."

"Who packed it?"

Morrell stared.

"*Jeffery*—and he was the only one to have a key beside myself!"

There was no sign of the brushes in Jeffery's bag, or in his study. Morrell telephoned the Park Lane house, sending a servant to look through his rooms there. But the brushes were not in the drawer Morrell would have used for them—nor could they be found anywhere else. Morrell seemed thrown off balance, but as far as Dawlish could see only because it was, as he kept repeating, so incredible a thing.

"Perhaps," said Dawlish. "Presumably Jeffery stole the brushes, and Jeffery has been murdered. It could be coincidence, but I don't think so. Morrell, there's no need for the local police to know about this connection, but the Yard will have to eventually."

"I—I suppose so." Sir Louis did not seem perturbed by that.

"Tell them—the locals—that I've been here, and if they're curious advise them to telephone Chief Inspector Trivett at the Yard."

"I will," said Morrell. "I assure you that I will."

Dawlish felt sick at heart as he reached the carriage-drive in front of the house. The cabby was sitting at the wheel and smoking, red-faced but curious. He had, it appeared, heard the shouting.

"A maid with hysterics," said Dawlish briefly. "Get me back to my car, please, quickly."

They were out of the drive when a police-car came along, and the cabby glanced over his shoulder at Dawlish, who remained expressionless. The cabby made a mental note to report to the police if he heard of any trouble at Morrell's house, and deposited his fare at the station. He was pleased with his payment, but he frowned after Dawlish as the latter drove off; and for the first time he saw the bullet-holes in the wings.

"*Strewth!*" gasped the cabby. "'Ere, I'm not sitting on *this*."

He revved his engine and drove to the police station, and there told a garbled story to a sergeant more impressed because of the call received from River Lodge. The sergeant told the Station Superintendent, who had already heard the 'murder', and he had a general call put out for Dawlish who was 'gonged' near the scene of the encounter with Jonathan Grey. Thus it was that he returned under duress to Staines—and there gave vent to his feelings in no uncertain manner—when he should have been at Brook Street.

For it meant that he missed the visit of Jonathan's brother.

And he felt afraid for Lady Betty.

It was not the habit of Lady Betty Lorne to feel afraid for herself. She was twenty-three; she was attractive even though she could not be called beautiful—despite Cunningham's opinion. She had a figure in a thousand, and a superb self-confidence, the better because it was in no way ostentatious. She had lived most of her life out of doors: the Somerset home of the Lornes was the brighter because of her. She was, in most folk's opinion, adorable.

When the man approached her as she waited for Andy outside Dawlish's flat, she was smiling to herself through memory of Andy's hardly coherent story of the two luncheon engagements. Poor Andy! He was seven years her senior, and yet seemed such a boy. . . .

"Excuse me, Miss."

The voice was ill-educated. The man who possessed it was

not a prepossessing specimen, although he was dressed in chauffeur's uniform. He had unpleasantly thin lips, she saw.

"What is it?" asked Lady Betty.

"Just keep quite still," said a drab voice from behind her, "and you need have no alarm, Lady Betty."

And then she *was* alarmed.

But as she turned she saw the gun in the hands of a man who seemed completely grey; and something in his expression warned her that he would use it. She felt paralysed, she could have cried out had she wanted to. And the chauffeur took the wheel and drove off smoothly, while the man in grey sat behind her.

After five minutes, and at Victoria, she managed:

"What does this mean?"

"Quiet, please," said the man in grey.

Ebury Bridge—Sloane Square—Chelsea.

They turned into a side street, and stopped outside a small house near the river. Above the roofs of the houses she could see cranes and the masts of a ship. She felt cold, and quite helpless, for the manner of the man in grey was frightening, even when he kept his gun in his pocket with his hand about it.

"Step out here, please," said the man in grey. "You will be quite comfortable, and it will only be for a short time. I hope," he added, smiling thinly.

She hardly realised that he was gripping her arm, as the door of the house opened and she was ushered into a narrow passage which served as a hall. She saw only the man who had opened the door: a beetle-browed, uncouth specimen who leered at her. But she heard another cold, flat voice say:

"Upstairs, Lady Betty—right up to the top—don't be afraid."

A gun was poking into the small of her back, and she was terribly afraid—more than she would be after she had had time to think, and to recover from the shock.

That did not happen until she was in a small attic room; a room with only one tiny window, fitted with thick plate glass. She stepped inside, seeing the old furniture—a brass-knobbed bedstead, a marble-topped washstand, an uninviting chair. Grey did not follow her, but murmured:

"It will only be for an hour or two—*if* Mr. Cunningham is wise."

And then he closed and locked the door.

It was some minutes before the paralysis left her, and she felt that she could think. The simplicity of what had happened appalled her. She began to reproach herself for not making a fight, but the memory of the voice and slate-grey eyes of her captor told her she had been wise.

She waited.

The hands of her wrist watch pointed to half-past four—five o'clock—six o'clock. She stood up and walked restlessly from wall to wall, but the minutes went by relentlessly and nothing happened: she heard no sound.

Until, at twenty past seven, she heard a voice—no longer monotonous, but vicious—say:

"The damned fools! They think I'm bluffing. They won't think so when I've finished with *her*."

And all the fear she had known before came back intensified. Terrified, she stared at the door as she saw the handle turn.

"*When I've finished with her.*"

The words echoed and re-echoed in her mind, even as the door opened and Lancelot Grey stepped in.

CHAPTER XIII

13 LISTER STREET

Bill Farningham preferred not to work on his own initiative, for he knew something of the weird and wonderful machinations of Pat Dawlish's mind. Ideas and suggestions which seemed crazy had a habit of becoming sane when Dawlish worked them out—and certainly he had been anxious not to go to the police. Yet it appeared to be a choice between a free-for-all with Cunningham and a word with Trivett. After Lancelot Grey had gone, without the brushes and with him an aura of colourless evil that was almost frightening, Andy said abruptly:

"Get the police after Betty."

"Old son, Pat Dawlish is as safe as houses."

"I don't give a damn what Dawlish said, this business is murderous—Betty's in danger! Are you going to phone the police, or—"

A loud ringing made him jump. Farningham picked up the receiver and heard Dawlish's voice:

"Developments, Bill?"

"Grey's been and gone, breathing threats against Betty. We'll have to do something, Pat—Andy wants to try the police."

"Do that," said Dawlish. "We haven't a chance in a thousand of finding those brushes in a hurry, so we must get busy in other ways. Try to get Trivett: if not, Morely. Describe Grey, and suggest the Chelsea area for concentrated inquiries—the Benz was stranded there. Discretion's essential. Clear?"

"Just about," said Bill resignedly, and pushed a hand through his dark thatch. "Where are you?"

"I'm under arrest," said Pat Dawlish with some heat, and rang off. He turned to the Station Superintendent who had, quite rightly, ordered his detention, and asked with withering sarcasm whether that gentleman would be so good as to inquire of the Assistant Commissioner, or Chief Inspector Trivett, as to the accuracy of his story.

The Superintendent was a man of understanding and did not take umbrage. Instead, he telephoned the Yard, and found the A.C. in. Morely confirmed Dawlish's story, adding:

"Give him all the assistance you can, Superintendent."

"Very good, sir, thank you." There was respect in the Super's eyes as he regarded Dawlish afresh. "Sorry, sir, but you should carry your credentials with you. Is there any way I can help you?"

"Lend me a police car and two hearty policemen," said Dawlish. "And a word in your ear. If it should be suggested that Sir Louis Morrell is watched for the next few days, either turn down the suggestion or make sure a really first-class man is on the job. If Morrell gets wind of a shadow, he'll raise merry hell— and he has friends in high places."

"I'm aware of that," said the Super ruefully, and pursed his lips. "*Could* he have—"

"He couldn't and didn't," said Dawlish. "Someone came in by the window and Morrell had the shock of his life. Now, about that car?"

He was in the driving seat of a police Zephyr five minutes later, the radio on. A sergeant sat next to him, and a C.I.D. officer just behind him. Neither commented as he drove Londonwards through the gathering dusk with a speed that seemed nightmarish.

Suddenly the radio gave tongue:

"*Calling all cars in C2 Division. Wanted man dressed in grey known to have entered house in Lister Street, Chelsea. Close on Lister Street, but await further instructions before entering. Calling all cars . . .*"

The man at his side had earphones as well as a microphone, and Dawlish snapped:

"Try to get me Chief Inspector Trivett . . . yes, Trivett."

He waited for ten seconds, during which time he swung the Zephyr into Chiswick High Street, and then his companion said: "The Inspector is on the air, sir," and pushed the mike towards Dawlish.

"What number Lister Street?" asked Dawlish, without introducing himself.

Faintly from the loudspeaker came Trivett's voice.

"Thirteen—Dawlish, what is it about?"

"Kidnapping or abduction; please yourself. Lady Betty Lorne is probably at the house: if the police are known to be converging there'll be only her spirit left. I'll be there in ten minutes. Have the place surrounded, will you, and get a pair of silver-backed hairbrushes so that I can pick them up at the end of Lister Street."

"*What?*" gasped Trivett.

"You heard. Beg, borrow or steal them, but have them there for me. It's urgent, old man—" Dawlish's voice was quieter and its grimness more effective. "And where, exactly, is Lister Street?"

* * *

Third turning right, past Lot's Road, then second left; it was near the river. Dawlish swung his wheel at the third turning right, and the dim lights of three police cars showed. He pulled up swiftly, and jumped out of the car. Trivett, a vague figure in the gloom, held out a small package.

"Bless you, Triv," said Dawlish. "The brushes might just do the trick. I'm going to Number Thirteen alone. But if you could have two or three men in the street—all armed, and ready for a rush if there's any shooting—fine."

Trivett knew his man too well to ask questions.

"We can get a dozen; they'll never be seen in this gloom."

"Two or three near the house, the others farther away," said Dawlish firmly. "Our gentry might have eyes in the dark." He grinned, but bleakly, and tore the paper off a pair of silver-backed brushes. "Wish me luck, Triv."

He walked off, and in thirty seconds turned into the iron gate of Number 13. He reached the front door in three strides, and rang loudly at the bell. There was a pause, and then the sound of a chain being drawn back. The door opened and a faint light showed the silhouette of a short, thickset man.

"Tell Grey I want to see him," he told him sharply. "And tell him I'm not alone. The name is Dawlish."

The man gaped—but moved back as Dawlish forced his way in, showing his gun. He waited in the narrow hallway, while the man went up the stairs.

And then he heard a girl's voice, raised but tense:

"You're *mad*! You'll never get away with—"

"We will see about that."

It was Lancelot Grey's voice, and Dawlish lost something of his own tension, for both Grey and the girl were here. He was well up the stairs when he heard Grey snap a question and the man who had opened the front door answer:

"A cove named Dawlish, Guv', he—"

"*Dawlish!*"

There was enough in the high-pitched word to make Dawlish realise that Lancelot Grey held him in considerable awe—but there was more. Grey was scared—and he would not have been scared had he had enough men in the house to feel safe against intrusion.

Dawlish reached the second landing and saw the open door, with the thickset man outlined against a brilliant light, and Grey just visible beyond him. He thought he saw the girl, but could not be sure. He had moved with the speed and silence which made him seem at times uncanny, and he was within two yards of the room before Grey saw him.

Grey's hand flashed to his shoulder.

"Oh, no," said Pat with surprising gentleness, and he fired from the waist, aiming for Grey's thigh. It would have been impossible to miss, and Grey gasped with the sudden pain and collapsed with the abruptness of a marionette. The other man swung round—and met Dawlish's clenched fist.

He yelped, and sat down abruptly.

While into fuller sight came Lady Betty Lorne.

She looked pale, yet to Dawlish very lovely; whatever had happened, whatever she had been through, she had not lost her self-control. The one queer thing, Dawlish noticed, was that the sleeve of her blouse—the right sleeve—had been torn away.

Dawlish saw the hypodermic needle then, and the small capsule near it—a capsule containing one of the more vicious drugs: of that he felt certain. In that moment he felt an almost berserk rage, but at the same time a cold, sickening fear. For Grey had been prepared to carry out his threat.

That seemed more important than the fact that Grey was on

the floor, moaning a little, and with blood seeping onto his grey trousers from the wound.

"Who—" began Lady Betty.

"Not just now," said Dawlish gently. "Have you seen any others, apart from these two?"

"Yes, there was one. A very tall man—"

"Right," said Dawlish. "He might or might not be about—we'll take the chance." Speaking, he bent over the thickset man and with complete indifference to the fellow's gasp of fear, hit him scientifically on the back of the head with the butt of his automatic. Betty stared, wide-eyed. Dawlish felt the unconscious man's pockets and drew forth a Mauser, repeating the trick with Grey, whose gun came from a shoulder-holster. Grey had stopped moaning, and the expression in his slate-grey eyes was far from pleasant.

"I'll be back," Dawlish told him. "Get behind me, sweetheart. I—but just a moment."

He knelt by Grey again and running his hands through the man's pockets, found the small leather case containing the phials of ammonia-gas. He grinned, not with humour.

"Getting forgetful, aren't I? But I'll be back for you."

He moved towards the door and Betty followed, remarkably self-possessed and clearly very capable. A girl to be proud of, thought Patrick Dawlish as he went downstairs cautiously, his gun raised and his ears alert for any sound. He heard none, and the street door was standing wide open.

"We'll be all right now," said Dawlish cheerfully, "and Andy will be pleased to see you."

And then he stopped.

He saw the thing coming down from the porch—or what seemed to be the porch—and he saw the red glow that followed it. He knew what it was, he knew he had only a split-second in which to act—and he acted. He swung round, threw his arms about the girl and crashed her down beneath him. And as the back of her head met the floor, an explosion came. A sheet of flame and a billow of smoke, and a gust of wind that thrust Dawlish three yards along the floor, dragging Betty with him.

CHAPTER XIV

MEETING OF MEMBERS

For some seconds Dawlish was too dazed to think clearly; was conscious only of the drumming in his ears, broken from time to time by what seemed like thunder. And then a piece of plaster crashed close to his head, and he realised then the main force of the explosion had gone upwards, and that the walls were probably unsafe.

He moved cautiously.

The girl remained motionless, and he believed she was unconscious. He doubted whether that was because of the explosion; his body had covered her too well. She had banged her head, of course.

Another crash a little behind him suggested the falling of bricks. Unsteadily, he got to his knees. But he found his head reeling: knew he could not lift Betty by himself. He wondered vaguely why the police had not yet arrived, and cursed the darkness—complete now, for what light there had been had gone with the explosion. As vaguely, he realised that a man had been on the roof, judging the moment to toss the bomb—for bomb it had been—almost too perfectly.

Wearily, he reached his feet. He had to lean against the wall for a moment, and felt the plaster crumple beneath his elbow. He licked his lips, and half-turned towards the door. Then for the first time he saw shadowy figures approaching cautiously, and realised why the police had been so long: they expected opposition.

"Enter, friends," he called, and more loudly: "You there, Trivett?"

Trivett was.

He led three men carefully over the heap of rubble which was all there was left of the porch and front door, while torches revealed the damage inside the hall itself. The door had been lifted clean off its hinges, and was lying across the stairs, smashed and drunken-looking. A litter of glass and broken bricks lined the hallway and the stairs, but most of it had gone over Dawlish's head, and therefore Lady Betty's.

"The—man on the roof?" Dawlish asked slowly.

"We've sent up for him, but it'll be difficult," said Trivett.

Lady Betty was being put into a police car, when Trivett led him into the street, Dawlish saw three torches, their beams converging on his head, while the Chief Inspector made sure there was no scalp damage before giving him whisky: Trivett was afraid of concussion, and wanted him to talk.

"That's better," said Dawlish, as the spirit bit at the roof of his mouth and his tongue. "Nearly nice work, Triv, I'm glad I got here in time. You'll find two gentlemen upstairs, I think, in an attic room." He was suddenly bleak. "Not nice people, Triv. They certainly use drugs. And Triv, I must have a spot of rest."

Dawlish passed a weary hand over his face. "Triv, I'm sorry but if you don't put me in a little car and take me somewhere comfortable I shall go light-headed. I can feel it coming on. Betty's to come with me. Her boy friend's at my flat and he'll be anxious."

"Don't worry," Trivett said, "I'll get you away."

"And go through this place with a fine tooth comb," said Dawlish. "Twice, preferably."

He grinned, but was glad of a supporting arm of one of the Staines men, who led him towards a car.

Lady Betty, he was assured, was not likely to be unconscious for long; her only injury was the heavy bump on her head. He half dozed as he sat in the back of the car with her beside him, yet serious thoughts still percolated through.

'The outer fringes', he had told Trivett. And he was unpleasantly aware that he had a great deal further to go.

The four men at Abraham Larramy's Wimbledon house were equally sure that Dawlish had no more than reached the outer fringes—with one exception, and Larramy did not confide in the others about that. He might be termed the centre of the association which Trivett and Morely had suspected to be in existence but had been unable to find. There were, however, four other centres: the three men with him, and one other who rarely attended what was called a Meeting of Members.

Larramy knew that if he saw one of the other trio in the street he would not recognise them.

They were disguised. Not cleverly, but effectively. The object of their disguise was simply to make sure that their real features could not be recognised, in consequence of which grease-paint was used too freely, and in two cases beards were too-obviously false. They were all in dinner-jackets, but since Larramy had never seen them in other dress and did not know whether the clothes fitted their figures or were padded, that did not help him a great deal.

They preferred a soft light, and they made a point of sitting with their backs to it, so that their disguised faces were in shadow, while Larramy's pallid skin and staring eyes were vivid.

Sitting at Larramy's desk, in the one-time solicitor's study, they smoked cigars, and in front of them were balloon-shaped brandy glasses.

They were like tailor's dummies, Larramy decided—not for the first time.

He was not frightened of them, but he was a little anxious on occasions. He did not know, for instance, how they came to get in touch with him in the first place, except that it had been through the elder Grey—and on the subject of the Members, Lancelot Grey had never been talkative. In all other things the Greys obeyed Larramy without question, but since the Members themselves had suggested he should not be too curious on that one subject, Larramy did not press the point.

He was making money, hand over fist, in amounts which at one time would have seemed fantastic. He carried out his operations in whatever way he liked, being entrusted with the prosecution of the various activities mooted by the Members. They did not so much assist as suggest. They were always urbane and friendly. They had never suggested that they could end Larramy's peaceful life abruptly: nevertheless they contrived to convey that impression frequently enough to make Larramy wary.

He did not know their names, and mentally thought of them as One, Two, and Three. 'One' was the man who invariably sat nearest the window, and whose beard and moustache were brown, although his hair was grey. He spoke little.

'Two' was the man who always sat in the centre of the trio; his beard and moustache, like his hair, were grey. He spoke more than either of the others, in a pleasant, well-modulated voice which somehow did not ring true.

'Three' was clean-shaven and black-haired. When he talked, it was to criticise anything suggested or done—and while his criticism was often blunt, it was always fair.

They had arrived twenty minutes earlier in a closed Daimler saloon driven by the clean-shaven man. They had been ushered into Larramy's study by a manservant who knew better than to ask questions, and after the brandy had been passed round, Two had asked for the weekly report. Larramy had just finished it, and was waiting for their reaction.

"It does not," said Two at last, "appear to be very satisfactory, Larramy; you have not even found the brushes."

"And were those methods employed to obtain them justified?" asked Three.

"The Greys did it," Larramy pointed out, not without malicious satisfaction. "It seemed all right, but they always overplay their hand. It would have been safe enough, though, if Cunningham had been Cunningham."

"An elementary mistake," drawled One.

"I don't agree," said Three. "The man was due to lunch with Miss Farrimond, and that seemed a certain identification. Either Cunningham cried off because of his new engagement, or he was afraid of trouble and went to Dawlish for help. Dawlish is an enterprising young man, with some kind of reputation for this business. He mustn't be allowed to continue his activities, of course."

"He's got nine lives," growled Larramy, his voice no longer studied. "The smart Alec ditched Kramm; you know what that means."

"Yes . . ." said One slowly. "However, it is quite time we began to show the police that we are really in earnest. It will do no serious harm. It will, moreover, keep them guessing. We cannot expect to get through without some setbacks. What matters is getting the brushes."

"Cunningham hasn't got them. If he had, we'd have 'em by now," said Larramy flatly. "Grey 'phoned a while back and said that Cunningham was in a blue funk—and I don't blame him. We took the girl, and that'll stir him up some more. Dawlish'll come after her, of course, and since he's working on his own—" Larramy laughed, not pleasantly: "Dawlish will be handled at Chelsea all right, there's no fear of that. I'll have plenty of men working on Cunningham for the brushes, and we'll get 'em before long." His feverish eyes roved from one man to the next. "Why are they wanted?"

"Don't worry about that," Number One told him easily. "That is our business, Larramy. Just get them quickly. Now—where is Miss Farrimond?"

"At a Nursing Home in Bayswater," said Larramy, "she can't talk for twenty-four hours or more."

"I see. Then she can be left. Now of the other matters, Larramy. Are the consignments arriving here without trouble?"

"*Quite* okay," Larramy grinned. "It's smart, that. I—"

"We know it is clever and effective," said One testily. "We need not go into that. Distribution?"

"No trouble," said Larramy. "We've three more agents, and they're all sound."

"Excellent. All right, Larramy, keep operating carefully—but if the need arises, be quite ruthless. Now, if you will leave us for a while, we shall send for you when we have finished."

Larramy went out with alacrity. But as the door closed, he scowled and stepped swiftly towards the stairs. In thirty seconds he was in a barely furnished bedroom immediately above the study. He crossed to a small rug lying by the side of the bed and lifted it, revealing a small loud-speaker beneath a sawn floor-board. Faintly, the voices of the trio floated upwards.

"The Whitehall experiments," Number One was saying, "appear to be fairly satisfactory. The police have discovered only two of the seven experimental efforts, which means when it reaches a wider scale we should be sure of at least fifty per cent success. Enough, I think, for our purpose."

Three spoke thoughtfully: "We could do with more. . . . Once we start in earnest, of course, it will have to be done quickly."

"Oh, don't worry about that," said Two. "A week will be enough for everything, and then—" he laughed lightly. "It should have a salutary effect on Scotland Yard as well as Whitehall. Do you know, I've yet to find a loophole in the organisation. Larramy does the rough work very effectively, and Cautald is undoubtedly clever at Whitehall. I—"

The speaker broke off as the telephone rang sharply. He did not lift it, but pressed a bell on the desk, a summons for Larramy.

Larramy hardly knew whether to be pleased or annoyed by the comment about his work. But his main interest was in the name Cautald. He had known that there was another section of the activities of One, Two, Three and the usually-absent Four and was sure he would benefit considerably if he knew more about the Whitehall operations.

He hurried downstairs. When he entered, after tapping, One was holding the telephone. Larramy took it with a nod, and grunted:

"Well?"

"Abe, old Grey's through; Dawlish got the girl. I tried to put him out but it didn't work—"

The breathless voice at the other end of the wire said more, but Larramy hardly heard him. His pallor, if that were possible, had increased, and the direct stare from three pairs of eyes behind tinted lenses did nothing to lessen his perturbation.

"Hold on," he snapped. Then: "Things have gone wrong at

Chelsea—Dawlish again. They've captured old Grey," he told the others, and was astounded by the oaths that sprang from the lips of the three men, and the words that Number One barked:

"They mustn't hold Grey alive. I don't care how you do it, but put him away. Find where they take him, blow the place to pieces if you must, but *find Lancelot Grey*!"

CHAPTER XV

"FIND LANCELOT GREY"

Still incredulous at their reaction, but eager to impress them, Larramy said crisply:

"Hallo, Schuster—where'd they take Grey?"

"He's shot, in the house."

"Where're you?"

"In a 'phone box a hundred yards away."

"Got a car handy?"

"Sure."

"If they take Grey out, see that you follow him: make sure where he goes. If you get a chance to rub him out, do it—we'll look after you. I'll have four of the boys with you pronto, and they'll bring a load of sky-high: Grey's got to fade, and no argument. Get to it." He rang off, lifted the receiver again and called a St. John's Wood number. "Aggie? Four of the boys and a load of sky-high: get them to Chelsea pronto and take orders from Schuster. Don't fall down on it—I'll be around myself." He hung up and started for the door. "It's as good as done, don't fret."

The Members had recovered their composure.

"I will 'phone here every half-hour," said Number One.

"Telephone a report here as soon as you can. Don't make any mistake, Larramy: this is important."

"It's done, I tell you." Larramy went out, and as he went he nearly banged into the black, rigid figure of Ma Finnigan. Her lips were turned back in a sneer, and she said harshly:

"Made another mistake, 'ave you? You're always running risks, blast you."

"Shut up!" snarled Larramy. "Is Sloane sober?"

"For once, yes."

"Send him down to the garage in a hurry, heeled."

She snorted her contempt of him, but she hurried away, while Larramy went to the garage and took out an Austin. By the time the engine was warmed a stout, red-faced man whose veiny nose and cheeks bespoke the heavy toper, had come from the side entrance of the house. A shapeless trilby was on the back of his head and his grey mackintosh was unbuttoned. He eyed Larramy owlishly.

"In a hurry, Abe?"

"I'll say we are—get in." Larramy was at the wheel, and as he started off he saw the closed Daimler of the Members turning out of the drive. At another time he might have been tempted to follow them, but all that mattered just then was to find Lancelot Grey.

Near Lister Street, fifteen minutes later, he slowed down. A match flared ten yards ahead of him, went out, and was replaced by another. In the brief glare, Larramy saw a long, thin man and the outline of a telephone kiosk. He pulled up opposite the man.

"Has he gone?"

"Ambulance just reached the house, Boss."

"The others here?"

"Yeah, I've give them the word; they're waiting. As it comes round the corner they'll walk in, I reckon."

"Get a hundred yards up the road and if the ambulance gets through, follow it. Get going," rasped Larramy, and as he spoke he made out the faint outlines of the four men who were sitting in a saloon car.

There was a waiting period that got on his nerves, then suddenly Larramy saw the ambulance. He struck two matches in quick succession. The engine of the saloon hummed and as the ambulance turned the corner the saloon drove alongside it for perhaps five seconds. There was a pause, and then the saloon shot forward.

"Flatten!" snapped Larramy.

Doc Sloane obeyed and Larramy went prone on the pavement, still watching the ambulance—now no more than a vague shape in the distance. Then suddenly it was flame! A burst that seemed to spread the length and breadth of the thoroughfare: red, lurid and angry.

Larramy buried his face in his hands.

The gust of wind from the explosion passed over his head, but pieces of debris flew about him, one smashing through the wind-screen of the Austin. But he took a chance, and peered up. The ambulance, or what was left of it, was on its side, and flames were licking across the roadway. Farther down he saw the closed car, on all four wheels.

"Let's get going," Larramy licked his lips: "I reckon that's put paid to Grey."

Sloane started, and peered through the gloom.

"Which one?"

"The old one."

"By heck, his brother'll raise hell—"

"His brother'll do what I tell him," snarled Larramy. "Don't waste your breath—save it for drinking."

And the two men rejoined their car, which moved swiftly and

unobserved into the darkness of the night. While Trivett, with three of his men, was hurrying towards the scene of the explosion, more than a little afraid of what might have happened.

Dawlish was in a peculiar frame of mind as he was driven to his flat. He seemed to be floating on air, without a trouble in the world. Yet at the back of his mind was fear of what was coming.

He could walk up the stairs of his own volition, and he went ahead of the policemen who were carrying Lady Betty. He grinned as he opened the door with his key—and saw Bill Farningham gape at him, incredulous.

"The news is good," Dawlish announced. "I—what's the matter with *you*?"

Farningham began to laugh. His humour was not shared by Cunningham, who had been drinking rather too much. The younger man bounded across the room and gripped Dawlish's arm.

"Betty—"

"Safe, but for bruises," said Dawlish. "She'll be up in a moment, you needn't worry. Meantime, William, perhaps you'll—"

"Oh, Pat!" gasped Farningham, as Andy rushed from the room. "The sight of you would—Come!" He broke off and led the way into the bedroom, where he opened a wardrobe with a full-length mirror.

Dawlish stared.

His trousers had disappeared, but for jagged patches about his thighs. He had one sock and two suspenders. His coat was in ribbons, but his collar and tie were hardly touched and looked spotless. His hair was on end, his face and hands begrimed.

After a moment or two he grinned wryly. "The fireworks did that, Bill. Be a hero and run me a bath, will you, and then ring the restaurant for some food so that we can eat in comfort."

There was some purpose in his speedy movement into the sitting room, and it was not unconnected with the noise of footfalls on the stairs. As Dawlish entered the room he saw Cunningham standing by the door watching the two policemen carrying in his eighth or ninth *fiancée*. In profile, he looked pale and exhausted, but to Dawlish it seemed that his eyes were very bright.

"This couch," Andy said quietly, and Dawlish said: "Wrong guess, Andy: the spare bedroom."

Cunningham took Betty from the others masterfully, carried her into the spare room and put her comfortably on the bed.

"I'll have a nurse sent over," Dawlish told him. "But she's right as rain—there's no need to worry about that."

Cunningham was quiet but tense: "I'll murder the swine who took her, Dawlish. I'll choke the life out of him with my bare hands."

"No histrionics," said Dawlish, amiably. "The only thing the matter with Betty is a bump on the head."

Andy looked affronted for a moment. Then a glimmer of a smile curved his lips. "Sorry, Pat. Rather knocked me over. I'll be good."

"I need you to be," said Dawlish. "There'll be plenty of action before this business is over."

"Your bath is ready, sir," called Farningham jovially.

"Don't forget the food," Dawlish told him. "And call on Sister Em again, for a nurse to look after Betty and put her to bed." He went whistling into the bathroom, a scarecrow figure, who, for all outward signs, beyond the rags and dirt, had not a care in the world. He continued to whistle in his bath, while he considered how the two silver-backed brushes he had taken to Lister Street might still be used to advantage. Or better still, exact replicas! . . .

But the urgent problem was the hiding place of the genuine pieces. Of course Jeffery might have had them, poor beggar— could even have been murdered for them. But why the particularly vile killing? Dawlish stopped whistling as he recalled the shambles at the Staines house.

His mind turned to contemplation of Sir Louis Morrell.

The trouble was, thought Dawlish, that no drug taker was consistent all the time. Did drug addicts help to distribute the stuff—in a major way, that was? He would have to ask Trivett.

Then there was Chloë—

He heard the telephone while he was rubbing himself down, and with a bath towel about his huge frame, he stepped into the living room. His arrival coincided with that of the nurse, a dowdy-looking middle-aged woman whose eyes sparkled behind pince-nez at the sight of Dawlish and his towel. He waved and smiled engagingly, sitting down abruptly when the towel nearly dropped as he lifted the telephone.

"Dawlish speaking . . . *What!*"

He listened grimly as he heard the story of the death of Lancelot Grey. The crook, the ambulance driver and two attendants, Trivett told him, had been blown to perdition in a matter of seconds. The utter ruthlessness of the killing appalled him, as it obviously had the Chief Inspector.

Trivett went on: "We must have your full story now, Dawlish—you must keep nothing back. Sir Archibald and I are coming over—now!"

That, thought Dawlish, was a reasonable thing to do. He was still feeling the effects of his not inconsiderable day, and his head was aching dully. But he was his genial self and by now, respectably clad, when the nurse came from the spare room to declare that Lady Betty was in bed, and conscious. Cunningham hurried in to her, and Dawlish allowed him five minutes, then tapped with unnecessary vigour and joined them.

"And now," he smiled: "We can be introduced."

"I have to thank you—" began Betty, as Dawlish considered what a lovely thing she was: a creature born to the open fields and the countryside. There was a vivid freshness about her, despite the ordeal of the afternoon, and an answering smile in her candid grey eyes.

"Thank me for nothing," Pat said, "I more or less put you into the hole—the least I could do was to get you out of it!"

"But *why* did *any* of it happen?" demanded Betty.

"Betty, it's Mystery with a capital M, and I don't think Andy knows much about it. The starting point appears to be the silver-backed brushes he's told you about. Convince our friends—and I think I can—that Andy hasn't the first idea where to find the brushes, and you'll hear no more about it."

"*Won't* I?" said Andy with spirit. "I'll see this thing through, Pat."

Dawlish eyed a sober-faced Betty.

"Has he permission?"

"I suppose so. It's not much use saying no."

"You're an understanding soul," said Pat. "And you're a lucky man, Andy. Before we feed—you can have a bite in here with Betty—those brushes, old man. Where did Chloë buy them, have you any idea?"

"Not the foggiest. I—half a mo', though: there was a name tag on the box, I remember. Those people in the Arcade—Misslethwaite, isn't it? A tongue-twister, anyhow. Does that help?"

"I don't know yet," said Dawlish, "but I will soon."

He was to know sooner than he realised. But meanwhile he ate, and was at the coffee stage when Morely came in with Trivett.

And while Dawlish mentally marshalled his facts, deciding what it was best to leave out, without arousing suspicion, Larramy reached the Wimbledon house and was able to report success, when the first telephone call came from the man he knew as One.

While in an upper room at the house, Doc Sloane—whose chequered history was no adornment to the medical profession, which had long since spurned him—was telling Jonathan Grey that his brother had been liquidated.

He had never seen hate so naked on any man's face.

CHAPTER XVI

SIR LOUIS MORRELL IS ANGRY

"As far as I can see," Morely began almost at once, "you've taken far too much on yourself, Dawlish. When we asked for your co-operation, we didn't put you in charge of the Yard."

Dawlish raised one eyebrow and suggested gently:

"Hadn't you best have the whole story, old man? But first— what time did you come to see me, Trivett?"

"About ten this morning."

"It was five minutes to, precisely." Dawlish continued to appear amused. "Morely, keep at the back of your mind the fact that what I've got to tell you has happened since ten o'clock. A trifle over eleven hours, in fact. Now—"

He told the story precisely, clearly, and without embellishments. When he reached the moment when he had seen the burning fuse of the bomb, he broke off and without a change of tone demanded of Farningham a tankard of beer.

He smiled at Morely.

"On the whole, thirsty work, old man. And before you comment, can I have the full story of the blow-up with the ambulance?"

Morely nodded to Trivett, who told what he could. Farningham had by then filled four tankards, and as they drank, Dawlish said thoughtfully:

"First obvious thing, Morely, is that these gentry are *not* afraid of consequences. We've met the really ruthless type so many people won't believe exist. The second obvious thing is that no one would go to the lengths these gentry have gone to get something that was not important. On those brushes turns the solution to this affair, I fancy. The third obvious thing is that Lancelot Grey knew enough to be dangerous to Pale-face or whoever employs Pale-face. And the fourth obvious factor—and clearly the most important—is that after some months of insidious activity relating to some nefarious plot, these people are prepared to come into the open."

Morely frowned and drank deeply.

"You are probably right, Dawlish. It's an amazing business. But had you advised Trivett when you first realised what was happening, you might have saved a lot of trouble. The Greys might have been apprehended, for instance."

"It could be," admitted Dawlish, "but I have my doubts. I wanted the Greys to believe I was after those brushes: I did not want my connection with the police known immediately, and I believed I could handle the situation up to a point. Directly Lady Betty was taken it grew even more urgent to find the brushes and try to work an exchange—or a bluff. She *was* in danger, you know," he added casually. "Had there been a normal police raid I don't think Grey would have thought twice about killing her."

Morely looked a trifle disconcerted.

"You may be right. But, Dawlish, you must co-operate more closely." It was more an appeal than an order, and Dawlish appreciated Morely's difficulty; having invited co-operation, he would not present a convincing argument to higher authority should Dawlish make a disastrous mistake. "However—where does your story lead you?"

"What happened to the man I knocked out at Lister Street?"

Trivett frowned. "He's at Cannon Row. I doubt whether he can give much information, and anyhow he's suffering from concussion."

"I can't know my own strength," smiled Dawlish dryly. "Well, that's one Grey and one roughneck accounted for, and the mysterious Bilson not likely to be serviceable for some weeks to come. Not too bad for one day. Also, those brushes mean something, and Chloë Farrimond *may* be able to help. I don't think so, but—" he shrugged. "I want to talk to her before you people do. She has a will of her own, and if she doesn't want to talk, she won't."

"She must be interrogated."

"Precisely. I'm offering to do it. For God's sake!" Dawlish showed in that moment how taut his nerves were: "don't spoil the one witness who might be useful! If she closes up, you've got nothing to use against her—you can't force information, even if it's there. I can handle Chloë."

"We can leave it for the time being," Morely hedged. "What was your impression of Morrell?"

"A nasty piece of work. What's yours?"

Morely smiled in spite of himself. "More or less the same. The Staines people are quite sure the Jeffery murder was done from the window. I suppose Morrell—"

"I'd swear on oath that he had the shock of his life," said Dawlish. "He might have put up a good act, I know; but he wasn't acting, he was real. We presume that Jeffery knew the importance of the brushes, and was killed after he stole them. *Ergo*—someone knew he had stolen them. Presumptive evidence, I admit, but we haven't much else to go on."

"Morrell would be likely to know anything his secretary knew about them," Trivett protested.

"That isn't by any means certain. Secretaries do have their little secrets." Dawlish yawned, and did not return to the subject. "Did you get much in the way of finger-prints at Chloë's flat?"

Trivett said: "Yours, Farningham's, and those of a man named Grayson—no others. Grayson is your Bilson—" He told Dawlish what was known of the criminal record of Mr. Grayson, and Dawlish's eyes narrowed.

"Our man, all right—and he's certainly dangerous, in a corner or out of it. Anyhow, he's carrying a .45 slug somewhere in his shoulder, which should quieten him for a while. There's just one other minor point, Morely—concerning drug-addicts. What's the general rule? Does a drug-taker help in distribution, or—"

Trivett frowned, obviously wondering what had prompted the question.

"In a small way, yes—but no one organising wholesale distribution is likely to take it. It's not impossible, mind you, but most men convicted of smuggling the stuff into the country wouldn't take it for a fortune."

"Nice gents. I—"

Dawlish broke off, for the telephone rang. He was sitting where he could stretch his arm for it—a considered position, Trivett knew. Dawlish did little things like that automatically.

"Hallo, yes . . . oh, yes, Millie dear, but . . ." his grimace suggested that he was not pleased by the interruption, and Trivett glanced half-humorously at Morely, who also assumed that it was a lady who felt lonely. "I know I was disgustingly rude, but I had to go away quickly, I . . . *what!*"

Dawlish sat up in his chair, his eyes a-gleam.

"What kind of man . . . you're quite sure? . . . and you told him that Sir Louis Morrell. . . ? Millie, you couldn't help it, I should have warned you . . . no, not really serious, darling, but I must go now."

For the second time that day he rang off abruptly on Lady Milhampton, and snapped to Morely:

"The other Grey's been at the Milhampton place, inquiring about the brushes. He knows Morrell bought them, and that's not good for Morrell. Get Staines."

"He's back in London." Morely was already on his feet. "He insisted on leaving Staines, claiming he had an appointment at the Black Out that he could not miss. Trivett, get over to the club. I'll telephone for others to go there at once." That Morely knew how dangerous this development might be, was proved by his expression.

Dawlish hoisted his large frame out of the chair and glanced at Bill.

"Get on some glad-rags, old man: our day's work's not yet done. I'll be ready in ten minutes."

"Dawlish, you're too tired—" began Morely.

"Never let it be said," beamed Patrick Dawlish. "In the course of duty I never sleep—and after all, I'm nearly a policeman."

But he yawned, and continued to yawn while he changed into tails. Morely left soon after Trivett, further discussion on the affair of the brushes postponed. Farningham hurried to his flat—three doors away—and in the spare-room, Cunningham sat quietly and without moving, while Lady Betty slept.

And Sir Louis Morrell, at the Black Out Club, was already getting angry.

He had been due to meet Chloë Farrimond for dinner at the Superb, but the Staines police had detained him so long with their questioning that he had arrived late. Chloë had not been there—nor, when he phoned her flat, had there been any answer.

At half-past nine, he left a message with the head waiter of the Superb and repaired to the Black Out, in the hope that Chloë had gone there ahead of him.

The table which he had reserved so often during the past six weeks was empty. It was set in a secluded corner of the Club, which was at the best of times a place of shade and shadow and diffused light. Crammed to capacity most nights, it was one of the few night haunts where membership was genuinely required to obtain admittance—no five- or ten-pound note could make a magic *open sesame*.

Alone at his table, Morrell sat motionless, one eyelid drooping. Those who knew him well would have recognised the signs of mounting ire. His right hand drummed on the table, his left hand held a cigar from which smoke curled unheeded into his eyes. Now and again he glanced towards the door, but Chloë did not appear.

Then Leonardi, the manager, short and sleek and immaculate, made his cat-like way towards the table. Morrell stared up at him, his expression insolent. He would resent inquiries.

"Your pardon, *M'sieu*, but a man inquires for you."

Morrell stared. "Where?"

"In the foyer, sir, he is not dressed for—" Leonardi shrugged. "He has a message of some importance for *M'sieu*."

"I'll see him," said Morrell abruptly. "All right, Leonardi."

The manager bowed and made his silent way to others who needed personal attention, while Morrell finished a glass of champagne before going to the door. He felt a hundred eyes on him, was conscious of the fact that Chloë had made him look a fool. There was no greater offence in the eyes of Louis Morrell. He was inwardly seething with rage as he reached the foyer, and it did not ease when a nondescript-looking man in grey approached him.

"Sir Louis, I have word from Miss Farrimond." The voice was colourless and drab, like the man himself, and Morrell paid no heed to the expression in the slate-grey eyes—eyes which seemed to reflect a burning hatred.

"What is it?" demanded Morrell curtly.

"This is somewhat public, Sir Louis."

"It is private enough for me," snapped Morrell. "She's all right, isn't she?"

The slate-grey eyes narrowed.

"Sir Louis, I hesitate to tell you—she is in a most difficult situation: Only at great risk was I able to come to see you. She is anxious to have word with you."

"Where can I find her?"

"At the Regal, I have my car outside."

"I'll get my coat," said Morrell. He sent for it while the man in grey waited patiently; donned it, and followed the man outside. He climbed into the back seat and the chauffeur let in the clutch—and as the car disappeared into Shaftesbury Avenue, Trivett arrived from the Regent Street end of the short street which held the Black Out and Dawlish and Farningham left Brook Street in the hope of reaching the club in time. They did not.

And Morrell was not driven to the Regal Hotel.

CHAPTER XVII

TWENTY-FOUR HOURS

Morrell, in fact, disappeared completely, as far as Dawlish and the police could trace. In all justice to the police, Dawlish was prepared to admit, they did most of the looking. It had not been difficult to learn that a little man in grey had called for Sir Louis and that they had driven off together. But no one knew the make or number of the car in which they had gone, and it was impossible to trace it. Trivett sent two men to the Park Lane house, but Morrell was not there and did not arrive. Nor was he at River Lodge. They tried his clubs and the homes of his friends, although without much hope—and their pessimism was justified.

"Only thing we can console ourselves with, old man," said Dawlish gloomily when Trivett 'phoned him, "is that we acted as fast as we could. Of course we should have been watching the Milhampton *ménage*."

"A very long shot," Tribett said. "What are you going to do now?"

"Sleep," Dawlish answered promptly. "What else can I do? And if I don't, I won't be able to get around much to-morrow. Have you put some men on Sister Em's nursing-home?"

"Yes, three."

"Good man. I've a brace of hopefuls there, they can come and look after the flat. Cunningham's staying here for the night. And Farningham; there's safety in numbers. Lady Betty'll be as fit as a fiddle in the morning, I fancy; she's still sleeping."

"All right. But, Dawlish—"

"Hmm-hmm?"

"Don't keep so much under your hat," said Trivett bluntly.

Whereat Dawlish grinned and wished the Inspector good night and slipped into bed. Farningham and Cunningham were proposing to occupy the settee in turns throughout the night, while Farningham 'phoned the 'Shop' and arranged for Frankie and Ben to remove themselves from Sister Em's— where there had been no trouble—and decorate Brook Street instead.

Dawlish saw no point in taking unnecessary chances.

There was nothing to report during the night, and he was not sorry: the hectic events of the previous day left him more than a little languid and possessed of a thick head. He brightened for breakfast, over which Betty presided, and as he had expected she was as fresh and vivacious as she might have been on any day of the year. After a good night's sleep, the affair of the previous afternoon was like a bad dream.

Cunningham was correspondingly more cheerful.

"Time we were up and doing." He loaded marmalade on to his toast. "What's the order of the day, Pat?"

"There is none," said Dawlish amiably. "Look at it evenly, old son, and you'll see that we've precisely no place to start from. Until Chloë is able to talk, that is. I'll slip over to see her this afternoon. For the rest, Trivett will be doing all the spade work, and we can't do a thing. Except take care." He smiled at Betty.

"What does that mean?" demanded Andy suspiciously. He had

recovered himself completely, and his voice had its customary deep and melancholy note.

"Bodyguards," said Dawlish. "Frankie and Ben have gone off to sleep, but two others are due to arrive at any moment. Known as Slim and Monty, I'm told. I'll introduce them to you before you go out, and be warned that they'll be on your heels all day."

Andy put his toast slowly to his plate.

"Oh, no, they won't"

"Oh, yes, they will. Unless you want another dose of yesterday's treatment of Betty." Dawlish smiled, but his eyes were serious. "Sorry, old man, but we can't take risks. Slim and Monty will be armed, they're capable, and they're trustworthy. What's more, they won't get in the way too much."

Andy started to protest again, but stopped as Betty said:

"How long is this likely to last, Pat?" She had fallen in with Dawlish and Farningham with an easy friendliness which Dawlish appreciated a great deal. "A week, a month, or a year?"

Dawlish regarded her seriously. A woollen jumper, high at the neck and long-sleeved, seemed to emphasize the attractiveness of an oval face, whose lips were a little too full, and whose nose a little too short, but straight and firm. Her eyes were the vital part of her: blue-grey in the morning light, wide-set and gleaming as though she found the world a good place to live in. Her brown hair looked golden where the sun struck through the window. Soon after waking she had 'phoned her hotel for some clothes; she was not going to be perturbed if she had to stay at the flat for two or three days, that was obvious.

A girl, thought Dawlish, to trust instinctively.

"A week, a month, or a year," he repeated. "I wouldn't like to prophesy, my sweet. But two or three days should see the end of it. Damn it, no one can last this pace for much longer. I'm in hopes, anyhow."

"Without the slightest grounds for hoping," said Farningham resignedly. "I can see Betty and Di mooching around town on their own while Andy and I run off on some dam' fool stunt you think's important. When you've known him a bit longer, Betty, you'll learn that when he's on the prowl you can't trust a word he says, and the wider his smile the murkier the trick he's putting over on you."

Farningham gave Dawlish a glance of good-humoured affection, not untinged with admiration: "But we'll get through, and with luck I'll have a couple of days left of my stay to have fun in."

"He oughtn't to be about," said Andy sepulchrally. "He's dangerous. I get him to take a luncheon appointment for me, and before I know where I am you're kidnapped, and—well, we won't go into that again." Andy smiled sombrely. "We're not going to be followed about, for all that."

"No?" Dawlish appealed to Betty. His eyes asked her to deal with the rebellious Andy, and her eyes said that she would.

After breakfast Bill joined Pat in his bedroom. while the others argued, but not hotly, over the table. Finally Andy grinned.

"All right, sweetheart—Pat gets you all sooner or later. He's the world's best at making the fair sex feel foolish. Maybe you're right, too: I don't want any more funny business. Odd, though, from start to finish."

"Let him handle it," Betty urged, a hand on Andy's. She frowned a little. "I'll admit, darling, I'll be glad when it's over. Absurd, but I don't feel safe."

"We'll be all right," Cunningham assured her. Yet she could not repress a feeling that he too was worried.

And when they left the flat half an hour afterwards Slim and Monty, large, light-footed and faithful, were on their heels.

Dawlish was telephoning the Yard—to learn there was no news of Morrell. Descriptions of Bilson—or Grayson—and of the younger Grey were circulated to the police, although Dawlish doubted whether much would result. The possibility that the couple had been seen by beat-policemen remained, however, and Dawlish lost none of his admiration of the system of the Yard. So few things were left to chance.

But this business was not normal.

With Bill, travelling together on the basis that two were safer than one, he visited Misslethwaites, in the Arcade. Yes, the sale to Miss Farrimond had been recorded—yes, two silver hair brushes—yes, exact duplicates were in stock—yes, thirty-two pounds ten shillings.

Should they deliver them?

"I'll take them with me, thanks," said Dawlish, and twenty minutes later he was back at the flat, examining the purchase. The brushes were plain, with ridges running round them, and along the ridge of one, Dawlish ran his forefinger. He was not surprised at a sharp *click!* at the middle of the brush, and the silver back lifted.

"Gosh!" exclaimed Farningham, "they—"

And then he stopped, and Dawlish stared; both men were rigid for fully thirty seconds, and in the eyes of Patrick Dawlish was an expression difficult to define.

For in the cavity revealed there was a small brown-paper package, sealed with red wax.

Slowly Dawlish lifted it out, broke the seals, and opened the paper. He expected what he found—the fine white powder which had earned cocaine the slang term 'snow.'

"Now I wonder," said Patrick Dawlish slowly, "why the assistant didn't show us the trick, my William? They couldn't have many little gadgets like that, could they? To be sold to approved customers, or any asking for a specific article, presumably. Thirty-two-ten—a stiff price for this kind of silver: it's little more than a shell. Old son, I'm now deeply interested in the firm of Misslethwaites."

"Trivett will be."

"Trivett?" Dawlish stared, and then patted Farningham gently on the top of his rumpled hair. "Little man, be your age. If I tell the Yard about this, they make immediate inquiries of the firm and they just get nowhere at all—the men arranging this business won't leave simple loopholes. We might pick up an assistant, some poor beggar who's either been frightened into doing this or takes the filth himself, and we're back where we were. One distributing centre closed up, perhaps, and a dozen others left open. But Misslethwaites of the Arcade! They've been there for two centuries."

"Ye-es," said Farningham uneasily. "I don't want to seem awkward, Pat, but you took a chance yesterday, and where did it land you?"

"I don't know yet," Dawlish mused. "You're quite right, Bill. By all the rules I should call them, but—no, we'll do a little sleuthing on our own. I'm just beginning to see many possibilities. I wondered a lot about those brushes."

"You're not going to tell me you expected *this*," protested Farningham.

"Expected, no. Hoped for, yes." Dawlish shrugged. "And I knew there was something in the original brushes. Pale-face was so anxious to know whether I'd opened them. I wonder what it was? I wonder what our friends put in them before Chloë bought the things? We're going to see Chloë."

They did see her.

The actress was conscious, but she looked up at them blankly, while the doctor assured them that she had shown no signs of recognising anyone, or knowing where she was. She was in a stupor often brought about by drugs, and there was no certainty that she would come round in any given time; all they could say—and Bill confirmed it—was that she would come round.

"Which leaves us Misslethwaites," said Dawlish as he and Farningham walked along the Bayswater Road. "I—Bill, I take it all back. Trivett knows about the silversmiths right away." He spoke sharply and quickened his pace towards his car. A little way beyond it was an Austin.

"Nothing if not consistent," murmured Farningham witheringly.

"Consistent my foot. I thought we were alone but we've been followed. If we were seen at Misselthwaites a warning's gone out already; any other stuff at the shop will be cleared quickly." They were near the station, and he paused by a telephone kiosk. "I'll 'phone Triv now. You take a cab, and when the Austin starts to follow me, you follow it. I don't recognise the driver, but—"

"I do," said Farningham, and broke step. "Yesterday's chauffeur, a thin-lipped swab I'd know anywhere. Pat, we're in the thick of it!"

"And how!" said Patrick Dawlish. Which was a remark not typical of him but expressed his feelings to a nicety.

CHAPTER XVIII

THINGS MOVE

"There isn't the slightest doubt in the world," said Dawlish. "I bought the brushes and they were full of snow. Farningham will confirm it, it's not simply a layman's opinion. And I was seen to go there."

"How long ago was this?"

"An hour, and if you leave it more than another thirty minutes they'll get the stuff out before you can find a trace," snapped Dawlish, who at times was impatient that the world did not move as quickly as he thought it should. "Meanwhile, I'm going for a car ride. Don't fall down on this, Triv, or I won't pass on another item if you put me under third degree."

He hung up and hurried to the car where Farningham was waiting.

"I'll drop you in Oxford Street, close to a cab rank," said Dawlish. "It will look more natural. Don't pick a respectable cabby, whatever happens."

Farningham grunted, and they drove off—with the Austin close behind them. The shadowing was so blatant that to Dawlish it seemed suspicious, and he wondered if another car was following the Austin. He slowed down to light a cigarette, and the driving-mirror revealed a Morris with a red-faced driver whose battered trilby hat was pushed to the back of his head.

"He doesn't look the type," Dawlish mused, "but he could have passed had he wanted to. Have your cab behind that Morris, Bill; it'll probably follow the Austin."

He put Farningham off opposite Selfridges, where he appeared to go inside. The Austin and the Morris followed Dawlish and, at a traffic block, Farningham brought up the rear. Dawlish drove through the side streets to Westminster, where the caravan remained unbroken.

"Two cars," mused Dawlish. "They surely can't be thinking of putting something across me in broad daylight. Or can they?" He drove, still swiftly, towards Victoria and pulled up outside de Mond Mansions. It was then that he thought again of Colonel Adams.

The Austin drove past, pulling into the courtyard of a second block of flats. The Morris followed Dawlish, and the driver climbed out. He was a florid-faced, genial-looking man who showed from his eyes and his mauve-tinted nose that he was a toper; and his eyes, thought Dawlish, were unpleasantly close together.

He had his mackintosh open and went a pace or two ahead of Dawlish, towards the entrance. On the steps he paused, and Dawlish heard him swear mildly.

"Damn, no matches." He turned, saw Dawlish and smiled widely; his voice was a trifle hoarse but pleasant enough. "Do you happen to have a match. I came out in such a hurry that I forgot mine."

"Yes," said Dawlish, and took out matches while the other opened his cigarette case, "of course."

What it was that warned Dawlish, the latter could not be sure. Everything was so innocent, so above-board, and at first he assumed that his man was merely making sure who he was. The sudden glitter in the little eyes, perhaps, made him move sharply to one side—and at the same moment he heard a soft *zipp!*

A tiny whisp of smoke went up from the cigarette case.

Dawlish saw alarm flood the other's eyes as he half-turned and started to run, but Dawlish shot a foot out and sent him sprawling. As he fell he swore, not mildly, and the cigarette case clattered to the ground.

Again Dawlish felt a cold, intense rage. It was so simple, almost fool-proof. A cigarette case fitted so that it could fire a bullet or something as effective; everything in broad daylight, no sound nor sign of a gun.

As he flashed his right hand to his pocket and pulled out his automatic, he spared a glance for the Austin. It was already moving, while Farningham's cab was swinging round in the middle of the road. The Austin made for de Mond Mansions, travelling at speed, and as it drew level with Dawlish he saw the driver take his right hand off the wheel. He saw the two stabs of bluish flame, and he flung himself sideways—but as he did so he realised the shooting was aimed at the man on the ground. In front of his eyes granite chipped from the steps; the man there winced, and Dawlish saw blood on his temple.

Dawlish fired.

He was not using a silencer and the bark of the shot echoed and re-echoed along de Mond Street—as did a second, a third. He heard the bullets strike the metal body, but the car went on without stopping. As it swung round a corner there was a squealing of brakes from the cab, and the driver pulled into the kerb—Dawlish could almost imagine what he would have to say to Farningham.

Dawlish leapt for his own car as Farningham jumped down, snapping:

"Look after this fellow."

He pulled the self-starter, went over a low wall and, as the Allard jolted across the pavement, stepped harder on the accelerator. He reached the corner and swung round on two wheels, sending a policeman jumping for his life. He saw the tail-end of the Austin swinging into Victoria Street and going left—towards the Station.

He would have been on its tail but for a post-office van taking a wide sweep as it entered the turning. It meant a crash unless he stopped—and even stopping did not guarantee he would escape.

He swung the wheel, missed the front of the van by inches, and then braked. The Allard leapt into the air. Three people passing by shouted in alarm, and jumped away. Tight-lipped, Dawlish kept control of the big car, weaving it in and out of the passers-by. Stopped at last, he saw the postman, four pedestrians and two policemen hurrying towards him, all patently bellicose: and he sighed.

But there would be no object in abruptness.

He let the pedestrians have their say, and the postman his, before the police arrived.

"Your licence, please," said the first constable, a youngish man who seemed prepared for physical violence. Dawlish did not know that it was Farningham's acquaintance of the previous day.

The normalcy of the words eased Dawlish's tension.

"Right, Constable. I'm dreadfully sorry, but I don't think there's any serious harm done." As he spoke he took his wallet out and extracted a card—a card Trivett had brought with him on the previous night, signed by Sir Archibald Morely. The constable frowned, for he had expected the red of a driving-licence, stared, and then stepped back a pace, his expression comically different.

"Thank you, sir. I'm sorry, but—"

"You're quite right," said Dawlish, and he handed the man his proper card. "If there are any claims for damage or shock or what-not, I'll look after them. I can't stop now."

"Right, sir. Clear away, there: don't crowd round—"

Dawlish heard the roar of disapproval from the quickly-gathered crowd, and agreed that it was justified. But he had to get back to Farningham quickly. He was by no means sure that the man he had knocked over had played his last trick—if, in fact, the match-borrower was alive. He left the constable to make the peace; causing more anger as he drove slowly through the crowd, forcing a dozen people to give way.

He reached de Mond Mansions; and he chuckled.

Farningham was squatting on the steps, with the dilapidated customer from the Morris coupé standing in front of him. Almost playfully Farningham held a gun in his right hand, while four people stood on the pavement, staring as though petrified and certainly afraid to move. Dawlish pulled up, and as he crossed towards the couple, he saw a figure move from the entrance porch of the mansions.

"What the devil's up *now*?" demanded Colonel Adams.

Farningham did not turn his head:

"Hallo, Colonel. You might bring this cove out a spot of whisky, he looks as though he'll fade right out without it. Hallo, Pat. No luck?"

"Luck!" said Dawlish. "There's no such thing. Sorry, Colonel, you seem to live in the centre of it, but you're really safe and sound. Can you offer harbourage for us? A quarter of an hour or more will do; we'll have our friend at Cannon Row then."

"I—" Adams looked startled. "Oh, well—" His smile returned, and he seemed to derive a boyish excitement out of the incident. His trim, military figure quivered with sudden mirth. "Mary'll be delighted—yes, come up!"

Dawlish looked at a man who—he was to learn later—was called Doc Sloane.

"You heard," he said. "Take it very carefully or something might go off. If you'll lead the way, Colonel."

Adams led the way, and the crowd slowly disappeared, while at Flat Number 2 of de Mond Mansions Sloane hesitated until prodded in the ribs by Dawlish. A maid looked startled at the sudden arrival of three strangers: Dawlish could almost imagine her hoping they had not come for lunch.

Through the open door leading from the hall, Dawlish saw a middle-aged woman standing with a letter in her hand. She was as tall as Adams, plump, well-preserved and smartly dressed in a knitted suit. As surprised as the maid, she yet contrived a smile.

"Hallo, Bob. What—?"

"I'll explain later, my dear. We'll need the lounge for half an hour or so."

Mrs. Adams nodded and smiled, and Dawlish flashed a returning smile, with:

"Cold better to-day?"

"Better—oh, the cold. But how did you—?"

"Your husband confided in me yesterday."

Mrs. Adams' puzzled expression cleared, and Adams smiled. Farningham still held his gun, but in his pocket. The prisoner had collapsed into an easy chair, and was staring blankly ahead of him. Not a prepossessing specimen, Dawlish decided; his lips were loose and slobbery, and trembled a little. His hands were shaking—and Dawlish saw that the nails were ill-kept.

"Whisky would be an idea," he said, "while I use the telephone. If I may?"

"Of course." Adams poured out whisky, and handed a glass to Sloane, who grabbed it quickly and did not ask for it to be diluted. He put the empty glass on his lap and continued to stare, continued to tremble, while Dawlish 'phoned the Yard. Trivett was out, but Morely was available, and Dawlish explained briefly.

"I'll send for him at once," promised Morely. "And Dawlish— Thanks."

Pat turned, to see Farningham swilling his glass round thoughtfully, Adams standing somewhat at a loss, and the prisoner sitting like a statue: he had not spoken a word since he had missed Dawlish with the trick-gun, which had not yet been examined: Dawlish had it in his pocket.

Doc Sloane looked all-in: and, Dawlish thought, afraid.

The big man wondered whether he should try to force information then and there, wondered whether he had made a mistake in not forcing his way into Chloë Farrimond's flat and utilising the sound-proof apartments for third degree. He would have done so but for the urgency of finding what had happened at Misslethwaites and a feeling that for the time being it would be wiser to do nothing to cross the police.

This was no impromptu crime-wave. There was an organisation ready and waiting to act with a ruthlessness which was appalling. There would be no quarter. Someone had wiped the blood away from Sloane's temple, which had been scratched with the flint thrown up by the bullet from the chauffeur's gun. But had the chauffeur had his way, this man would be dead.

To prevent him from talking—

Just as the older Grey had died.

It was less the things that were happening than the speed and relentless efficiency of them that worried Pat Dawlish. There was barely time for breathing. A morning that had promised little had developed with the same crazy speed as the previous day. There was time for doing nothing thoroughly; one job was hardly finished before the next began.

But *could* this fellow talk?

Dawlish stepped towards him, and the close-set eyes of Doc Sloane stared up at him furtively. Dawlish heard his sharp intake of breath and knew how frightened he was. But as he stared he saw something else. The nostrils of the bulbous, purpled nose were pale and they twitched a lot; there was no surer sign of the snow-taker who sniffed his poison.

Sloane needed a shot of cocaine just then—as Morrell had needed one earlier.

Sloane, therefore, was close to breaking-point.

"I'll chance it," Dawlish said aloud, and he swung round on Colonel Adams. "Change of plan, old man, sorry. I'm going to take this gentleman next door, but we might be back before the police arrive. If not, refer 'em to me." He smiled bleakly, and moved his gun towards the prisoner. "Up, and look snappy!"

Sloane licked his lips, stared at the gun, and stood up slowly. He tried to speak, but no words would come, and Dawlish told himself he had never seen a man in a worse state of funk. Farningham opened the door; Dawlish gripped the prisoner's arm and led him into the passage.

"You didn't, by any chance, get a key of Chloë's flat?" he asked Bill.

"No, what's the idea?"

"It's question time," said Dawlish shortly. "Hold our friend while I look at the lock."

It was not going to be easy to get into the flat, he saw, and he wondered whether he would have time before the police arrived from the Yard. He had taken a skeleton-key from his pocket and was starting to probe at the lock when Farningham exclaimed— and on his cry there came a dull thud. Dawlish swung round.

To find that the prisoner had crumpled to the floor, was lying there with his lips wide open and his eyes staring. He was not dead—

But he died within three minutes and before the police arrived.

CHAPTER XIX

HOW DID HE DIE?

Apart from those few minutes while his breathing became shorter and more laboured, and his eyes stared as though he was already dead, the man gave no sign of pain or suffering. It was Farningham who confirmed that he was dead, and the medico stepped back from the body, his face gaunt.

"Heaven knows what it was," he said. "Poison, of course—"

Dawlish said softly: "But how did he get it?"

"Probably killed himself. I wondered what was the matter with him, he looked as if he was too scared to breathe in Adams' flat."

"Well, we'd better leave him here, we won't load the Adamses with corpses. Nice woman, that." He brushed his hand over his forehead, and his eyes looked lack-lustre: there was an ache at the back of his head that worried him, although he made no comment on it. "Right back where we started from, old man; we keep getting there. I wonder how the fun's proceeding at Misslethwaites?"

"You'll learn. Have a call put out for the Austin?"

"No use; he'll either strand it or change the number, these gentlemen have everything. By the way, your cab—"

Bill grinned. "The driver's language was lurid. I soothed him and paid him off. But never mind the cab. I—"

What he was going to say was never uttered, for a police car drew up outside de Mond Mansions. Among the three men who stepped from the car was a short-looking, burly, belligerent gentleman, by name Munk. Munk was Trivett's regular *aide*, a sergeant who had been transfered—at the time of Dawlish's first affair—from Guildford to Scotland Yard. He was a suspicious individual, and he had a not unnatural distrust of Pat Dawlish, for he believed in regulations and the letter of the law. Dawlish knew him as a friend as well as a subordinate of Trivett's, and knew also that Trivett could do no wrong in Sergeant Munk's eyes.

Dawlish went to meet him.

"Quick work, sergeant. I'm glad you've arrived. You're in time to take him to the morgue."

Munk glared. A spiky moustache, well-waxed, and baleful blue eyes were the chief characteristics of his florid face, which was square and chunky.

"No joking, *if* you please."

"Plain, sober fact," said Dawlish. But he had some trouble in convincing Munk of the manner of the prisoner's death. He could not blame the sergeant for being sceptical, although Munk irritated him beyond measure. Dawlish felt that it might be the headache which was at the root of the trouble. He knew how a 'morning after' felt but he was rarely visited by the dull ache which worried him that day. It was an effort to be civil.

There was not time for talking; that was the trouble.

Munk wanted everything in apple-pie order requesting full details from start to finish. To Dawlish, the murder of the prisoner seemed no more than further proof of the ruthlessness of the organisation he was opposing; in itself it meant little.

But there was no point in antagonising Munk unnecessarily.

He even made the pointed moustache quiver in a smile before Munk had finished, and with that evidence of better humour he said with emphasis.

"And now, Munk, I've got to leave it to you. Get hold of the local beat-policeman. They'll give you part of the story, and if you should find that Austin you'll be famous overnight. For the moment, I must get to Inspector Trivett."

Munk raised no further objections, and was left to superintend the removal of the body to the Cannon Row morgue—Cannon Row was in a different police division from de Mond Street, but the nearer the Yard the better it would be. Dawlish had advised that a pathologist conduct a *post mortem* immediately, and made a mental note to suggest the same thing to Trivett.

With Farningham beside him, he drove quickly towards Piccadilly. Nearing the Arcade, there was a traffic block of considerable proportions, a fact which did not surprise him immediately. The motorists were tolerant, although several were standing by their cars and staring ahead, as if trying to find the cause of the trouble. Equally puzzling was the absence of pedestrians from the Circus end of Piccadilly.

"Odd," Pat said.

He heard the sound then.

There was little doubt of what it was, despite the humming of car engines about him. There was a burst that lasted for ten or twenty seconds. *Tap-tap-tap-tap. Tap-tap-tap-tap.*

"My God!" Dawlish exclaimed. "Machine-guns. Bill, let's get out of this block somehow."

There was a sudden hum of voices raised in alarm. As he squeezed his way between the waiting cars, a policeman approached him, severe of aspect.

"Can't leave your car there, sir."

"I can and am doing," said Dawlish testily, and showed his identity card. It worked as it had done with the first policeman.

"Sorry, sir. Rather a mess up there."

"What kind and where?"

"In the Arcade, sir, I haven't been near enough to tell which shop. Thirty of forty of our fellows are there, sir, and I've heard they're rushing a company of troops over."

He stared: Dawlish looked the type of man who would be affable, yet Dawlish pushed past him and hurried through the thickening crowd, with Farningham on his heels. As they drew nearer to the Arcade the going was more difficult, and Farningham tugged at his coat.

"What is it?" demanded Dawlish. "I'm in a hurry."

"A copper would get us through quicker."

Dawlish's smile flashed. "Sorry, I'm not myself. Find one—ah. Constable—" he shouldered his way towards a policeman towering above the crowd, a crowd comprising men, women, and here and there children. A set, worried face looked into his, and Dawlish showed the card.

"Yes, *sir*?"

"Get me through to the Arcade in a hurry, will you."

"I'll do my best, sir. Move aside there, make way there—" The man bored into the crowd as to the manner born, squeezing through gaps which did not appear to offer any chance of passage. Dawlish and Farningham followed, making surprisingly good progress. There were a few curses, but little serious criticism, while the Arcade drew nearer, and:

Tap-tap-tap-tap. Tap-tap-tap-tap!

It was much louder now, and there remained not the slightest doubt that machine-guns were in use. Or one machine-gun. Dawlish knew what it was, told himself now that he should have expected it. He thanked the Fates that he had been grimly serious when talking with Trivett.

Ahead of him he saw a dozen steel helmets, with here and there a policeman. Closer, he saw that there were policemen making a cordon against which the crowd was surging. His constable reached the cordon, and way was made for them close to the entrance to the Arcade.

Dawlish's lips tightened, and Farningham exclaimed aloud.

Behind packing-cases and two cars, were a dozen policemen, three at least of them with guns. Others crowded in shop doorways, with several plainclothes men all looking along the Arcade. Dawlish recognised the Assistant Commissioner and a Superintendent named Wrigley: a large, impassive, fair-haired man.

As Dawlish made towards the A.C., there was another burst of shooting. Bullets struck against the tops of the cars. The police returned the fire, and Dawlish realised that they were using silencers, which explained why there had been so little noise farther along. But he gave it hardly a thought, he was filled with a sickening realisation that much murder could be done, and might be, before this affray was over. There were men of the Pale-face organisation here, of course, men prepared to die shooting if need be. At Misslethwaites, the most reputable firm of gold and silversmiths in London!

"Morely—"

The A.C. turned, and his set face lightened for a fraction of a second, a not unpleasing fact. He stopped in the middle of a sentence to Wrigley.

"I'm glad you've made it, Dawlish."

"How long?"

"Twenty minutes or so." Morely rubbed his chin, and seemed as though he had something to say but was reluctant to say it.

"Several of our men got through, but directly they inquired about the brushes this started. Two were shot in the shop itself, and if Trivett hadn't brought a strong force with him the men would have made their escape. As it is—" Morely shrugged— "they're not going to be taken alive."

"Which at least means we're moving. Where's Trivett?"

Morely said slowly:

"In there. Alive or dead I don't know, Dawlish. He was one of the first in, of course, and the only man who got out said that he was alive the last he saw of him. But God knows whether he is now."

And Dawlish knew that Chief Inspector Trivett stood little chance of getting out alive, if he were not already dead.

CHAPTER XX

STATE OF SIEGE

There was, Dawlish realised, no use at all in blathering about having to get in. From the porchway where he was standing he could see the barricade, hastily erected and yet obviously ready for such an emergency, which had been put across the doorway of Misslethwaites. Through it he could see the muzzle of one Tommy-gun, and he would not have been surprised had there been others. He scowled suddenly, for he caught a glimpse of a man inside the open doorway of the shop—unrecognisable, because he was wearing a gas-mask.

"Yes," said Morely, "they're prepared for anything short of being blown to pieces, and we can't do that. We might starve them out: it depends how well they're prepared. We'll use the fire-hoses, but I doubt whether it will be effective. They mean to stay."

Dawlish stared: "You're resigned to it?"

"I can't be anything else," snapped Morely. "They've a dozen assistants inside—genuine men who know nothing about the drugs, that's reasonably certain. There are offices above, all filled with people. They've taken command of the entire building.

The roof is guarded with machine-guns, and so are the upstairs windows. I've checked everything and there's only one conclusion possible—they're prepared for a long stay."

"But in the long run—"

"Yes, I know," said Morely testily. He looked as if he were disappointed in Patrick Dawlish. "We'll get them in the long run all right, although we don't know how and we don't know what's going to happen meanwhile. We *can't* use anything heavier than machine-guns against them for fear of killing others, and gas will be useless. It's fantastic."

Dawlish rubbed his hand over his fair head.

"It can happen, of course. So many things can, when we see them in front of us. And Trivett's in there."

"He is."

"Bad," said Dawlish, and he seemed to talk like a schoolboy. "Damned bad. Why? What makes it worth it? Why stage this kind of a Sidney Street stunt in Piccadilly when—" he shrugged, and smiled lopsidedly, "If Chloë's brushes contained anything about this place, it might explain a lot."

"Damn the brushes!" snapped Sir Archibald Morely, and turned away abruptly. "You're quite sure nothing's been overlooked, Wrigley?"

"Every point has been tested, sir. There's no way of getting into that building without meeting a barrage of machine-gun fire."

"All the same, Morely, I think I might get in," said Dawlish, apologetically. "With luck, that is."

Morely stared: "What crazy notion have you got now?"

"Those things you damned," said Dawlish slowly. "The brushes. There's a set in my car which looked suspiciously like the real ones, I gather, and the leader of the gentry in there might be prepared to take risks to get his hands on them. The car's half-way down Piccadilly. Allard, black, XC123X. If you could have them brought here, I'd be glad. They're in a cardboard box."

"Send two men for the box, Wrigley," Morely ordered clearly, prepared to try anything. "I don't think there's a great deal of chance, Dawlish."

"No," said Dawlish, and felt better than he had all day. His eyes were clearer, and his lips were smiling—which was typical of Pat Dawlish, who had a habit of doing the thing least expected of him. "But while we've the brushes we've hope. I wonder if anyone else could be in there?"

"Meaning?"

"Well, Morrell. He disappeared, you know. And Pale-face. It *could* be the headquarters, when all's said and done. Why so sure that there are non-combatants in the shop, old man? They could all be in the swim, you know."

"I don't think they are," said Morely. "There are twenty-one assistants in the showrooms, and a clerical staff of eleven upstairs, on the first floor."

"Goodly numbers, yes. They're quiet."

On his words came a further burst of machine-gun shooting, and granite chipped out of a pillar close to his waist. Panes of glass were suddenly starred with bullet holes. The burst of shooting lasted longer than any of the others, and in the middle of it Dawlish said:

"Could there be a gas-mask?"

"Well, if you—"

"I do," said Dawlish. "Incidentally, they're prepared against gas, and your men aren't."

"You're suggesting—?"

"I'm not suggesting, I'm telling you that we'll have a gas attack, and quickly." Dawlish spoke sharply, tensely. "They're bound to try to make a break. I—for God's sake, man, have the neighbourhood cleared! There'll be hell to pay if you don't."

Morely said slowly, "I've given instructions—but we've been working on the assumption that they're prepared to hold out for a while. They'll never try to break through: they'll know it's impossible."

"I wish I thought so," Dawlish retorted. "Damn it, what purpose can they have in just holding out? None, Morely, none at all. But if they *look* as if they're digging themselves in, they'll have an easier job when they make their sortie, especially if they use gas." He rubbed his large chin thoughtfully, and saw the doubt in Morely's eyes. "I hope the brushes will be here in time to hold things up, but I wouldn't be surprised if they're not. Anyhow—gas-masks!"

Morely beckoned a sergeant, who was sheltering nearby, gave him instructions and sent him off.

Masks were soon issued to all those within the barricade who could be safely reached and an uneasy silence fell. Unavailingly, the police tried to disperse the curious crowd.

The first intimation they had was when a policeman behind the car nearest the shop threw up his hands and collapsed: there had been no shooting at that moment, and no sound. Then a second man did the same, and Morely shouted:

"Gas! *Gas!*"

Dawlish had never seen panic like it, and hoped he never would again. The wave of gas went beyond the police and the barricades: people began to scream, and a stampede started in the section of Piccadilly opposite the Arcade. It had been crammed with sightseers with hardly room to move, and now they tried to get away while the waves of gas swept on towards them; insidious, unstoppable. The screaming was like bedlam, and for those few minutes there was no one to stop the panic, for the police were caught as swiftly as the people. Dawlish could not see Morely's features but he could imagine his feelings—knew he must be in hell.

The worse because he could have avoided it.

Yet no one, normally, would have expected this. Dawlish's cold logic alone had reasoned the only way in which the men inside Misslethwaites could possibly get free. By creating panic—*and then joining the crowd.*

The screaming reached a high pitch that was horrible to hear. The police turned towards the crowd in the hope of making some order out of the chaos. Along Piccadilly the people went in droves, some silent but most screaming—and those who could not make the pace went down and were crushed.

Morely went towards Piccadilly, heedless of possible bullets from the show-rooms, thinking only of trying to take command. Farningham began to follow, but Dawlish's hand closed about his friend's arm.

"Wait," he said.

The tension in his voice was not wholly because of the distorting effect of the gas-mask, and Farningham felt a chill shiver run up and down his spine. Dawlish looked grotesque as he stared towards the barricade, but obviously he was waiting for something, perhaps some new horror.

Tap-tap-tap-tap.

"No use," Dawlish said, and within him his heart was like stone. "Get ready to fall, Bill."

"But—"

"Fall!" cried Dawlish, and he flung himself downwards.

Farningham did the same, and was in time—but few were able to avoid the blasts of the explosions that followed. Four separate bombs were hurled from Misslethwaites towards the police barricade; four flashes of flame, four explosions in quick succession, echoing in a continuous roar. The screaming died away, deadened by the repercussions; one of the police cars seemed to break into a thousand pieces, and each piece flew towards the crowd. Something thudded above Dawlish's head; there was a crash as it hit the door behind him. A window went in, bricks and mortar crumbled—

And then the rush started from the show-rooms.

Dawlish was still on his stomach when the first of the men came through, but he was in time to see them reach the crowd. All masked, all of them armed, they were moving swiftly under cover of a barrage of machine-gun fire from the shop itself. A dozen men—

A *dozen* men—

Two dozen, three—

Dawlish did not use his gun. Shooting would draw the machine-gun fire towards him and Farningham: it was only another way of committing suicide. He knew there was nothing at all that he could do, knew that the men would get away. Had he been sure which were the most important he might have taken the risk, but if he fired he knew he would only be likely to hit another such as Bilson—a man whose place could easily be filled.

Farningham was muttering inside his mask, the words incoherent. Dawlish felt like ice as the last of the men left the shop. It had all been done so quickly and efficiently that less than two minutes had passed, and the first men were already mingling with police and people: could not be distinguished in the crowd. They were free, they would get clear away; nothing could stop them.

Dawlish saw no one who might have been the pale-faced man of Chloë's flat, no one who might have been Sir Louis Morrell. If there was anything of interest in the men who left the shop, it was that few of them were tall.

The noise of the crowd, farther away, seemed of little importance now. Morely might have gone in the explosions, dozens certainly had: he could see the battered, broken bodies of some of the victims, and he felt sick. It was a shambles, and it could have been avoided—and yet Morely had done what most men would have done.

No one to blame—

He stopped thinking, and touched Farningham's arm. Together they went towards Misslethwaites; there was no opposition as they went through the gap in the barricade. The shop was dark inside, but several figures lay on the floor, all motionless.

Trivett?

Dawlish reached the first man and knelt down. He did not recognise him, but knew that he was dead. The second—

Dawlish jerked up, startled beyond speech. For the pale face that he saw was that of Andy Cunningham. Andy, here!

He had a mental picture of Lady Betty, and for her he felt afraid.

CHAPTER XXI

WHERE DID THEY GO?

After the first moment of surprise, Dawlish pushed all thought of questions and answers from his mind. He lifted Cunningham easily from the floor, resting him in a nearby chair. There was no gas in the sale-room as far as he knew, and in any case Andy would have had his fill of it had there been any inside Misslethwaites.

Andy was breathing.

His pulse, although fluttery, was clear enough and Dawlish did not call Farningham, who was on his knees beside another man stretched flat on the floor. As Dawlish approached he recognised Trivett's drawn face—and rapped:

"Is he dead?"

"He'll be all right," said Farningham. "It's a knock-out gas, but it doesn't seem to be doing any damage beyond that."

"Humanitarian methods," said Dawlish ironically, more relieved than he realised by the safety of Trivett. "Did Andy tell you he was coming here?"

"Andy?"

"Did he?"

"Good Lord, no! I thought he was going out with Betty. Pat, he's not—"

"No worse than Trivett," said Dawlish. "I'm liking this less and less, Bill. I'd have said today that where you found Andy, you'd find his lady. No woman left the shop, that's reasonably certain; and if it's true, we might find her here. If it isn't—"

He stopped, and his face was savage: "Damn it, the telephone!" He saw one at once, and grabbed it. Then he scowled; there was no life in the instrument.

"They didn't intend to take chances. We'd better get everyone we can find into this room—by then, things will have settled a little outside."

He broke off, for the next man he saw was dead: shot through the head. Dawlish recognised his face, that of a C.I.D. man. Moving heavily yet with deliberate speed, he and Farningham brought the seven living men they found in Misslethwaites to the front sale-rooms. The seven had all been on the ground floor; the offices on the first floor were empty. What was more informative was the fact that filing-cabinets and desks had been opened, and as far as Dawlish could see most of their contents had been removed. It was another lesson in the thoroughness of the organisation he was fighting and did little to encourage optimism. He felt as if the things he had seen that morning were part of a fantastic nightmare, and yet all about him was the evidence of its actuality. As he worked, he felt a nagging anxiety at the back of his mind for Lady Betty Lorne. . . .

That this business could have started because he had bought a set of hair-brushes, seemed absurd—and it was certainly absurd that he should blame himself for the disaster. He did, nevertheless. Had he only guessed the importance of Misslethwaites to the organisation, it could have been avoided. In the first rush of revulsion to the mass attack on the crowd and the police he had been inclined to blame Morely: *he* was to blame, not the Assistant Commissioner.

A shadow darkened the doorway of the shop as he helped Farningham roughly bandage the head of a C.I.D. man who had been shot but was still breathing. Dawlish glanced round—and saw Morely, huddled in a mackintosh several sizes too large for him, his face streaked with grime, and his right hand held upwards: the two middle fingers were lacerated badly.

But at least Morely was alive.

"What have you found?" he asked in a dead voice that worried Dawlish more than the injured finger. "Anything?"

"Not much," said Dawlish. "What's it like outside?"

"It's—unbearable." Morely pushed his left hand across his forehead, and then straightened his hair automatically. "Two or three dozen men and women are—oh, my God!"

"Easy," said Dawlish, and from his hip pocket he took a flask. "Have a spot, old man, and then Bill will repair those fingers." He led the A.C. to a chair, and it said much for Morely's state of mind that he obeyed without question. In his eyes there was a haunted look, the expression of a man who had seen—and perhaps was seeing—horrors.

Farningham spoke brusquely.

"We'll soon put that right, Morely—rest your arm along the side of that case." The case was a long one of glass, and inside were a dozen pieces of silver, exquisitely worked, but none of the men noticed them.

Dawlish stepped heavily into the Arcade.

A dozen policemen, apparently unhurt, were moving the wounded and dead from the barricades. Three of them were working without gas-masks, and as Dawlish entered the Arcade two others removed theirs. Dawlish followed suit. The air was fresh enough; obviously the gas had dispersed quickly.

Quickly? A glance at his watch showed him that it had turned half-past two: he had been inside the sale-rooms for over an hour. Time did not seem to count. He went into Piccadilly, and there he saw squads of police and troops lifting injured men and women into ambulances. On the pavement were motionless bodies laid out, not yet covered with sheets. Three groups of men were carrying stretchers, also to the pavement. A lane had been cleared along the centre of the roadway, and other ambulances were coming to the scene of the disaster.

The crowd had kept back, and except for stranded cars and the victims of the stampede, only official workers were in the immediate vicinity. Dawlish stood still, his hands in his pockets and his expression almost hopeless. He had escaped with little damage to his clothes, but he was covered with dust and smoke, while there was a jagged tear in his sleeve where a piece of shrapnel had torn through it. As he stood contemplating the horror of a scene that might have been a battlefield, a Rolls was driven into the cleared area, and he saw the Home Secretary and the Minister of Defence step out. Both men stopped short when they saw the devastation, and for the first time a smile curved Dawlish's lips.

It would not be long, he believed, before he saw them again.

But he hoped to find Betty first.

Lady Betty Lorne was not at her hotel, nor at Dawlish's flat, nor at Cunningham's. She appeared to have disappeared with even less trace than on the first occasion, and to Dawlish it seemed a fortunate thing that Cunningham was still dazed by the effects of the gas—a gas which had not yet been identified.

It was an incoherent story that he told.

He had been with Betty to one or two shops, and on the way discussed the brushes. An idea, he had thought, would be to buy a set exactly the same as those he had given away. Betty had disagreed, but Andy had been obstinate: Betty, consequently, had gone to another shop in the Arcade—without specifying which—while Andy had gone for the brushes. He had not been inside for more than a minute when Trivett had entered; and the next thing he knew he had been struck from behind, and had remained conscious only long enough to know that a gas pistol had been used, with the gas forcing its way into his nostrils. He believed Trivett had been treated in the same way.

He looked at Dawlish dully.

"Sorry, old man," he mumbled. "Shouldn't have, of course, but I was damned anxious. I—you'll find Betty, won't you?" For the first time he showed some kind of animation, and Dawlish responded far more cheerfully than he felt.

"Lord, yes, it's as good as done! I'll get on the go at once."

"Where am I?"

"Still in Piccadilly, they've used some empty premises for a field-station." Dawlish smiled, glanced at a nurse who was with Cunningham and three others—the other three unconscious—and went out. Farningham was in the hallway outside the room, and as Dawlish joined him Det. Sergeant Munk came in from Piccadilly. A dejected, shocked-looking Munk, whose pointed moustaches drooped; he created the impression that he did not believe what had happened.

"Well, Munk," said Dawlish. "Messages?"

"Yes—yes, sir. Sir Archibald's compliments, and will you please go to his office at once? I've got a car outside," added Munk, as if casually. "I'll give you a lift."

"Why not admit you came for me?" Dawlish said, and smiled.

"What if I did—strewth, Mr. Dawlish, how the 'ell *can* you grin like that now?"

"Will crying help?" asked Dawlish quietly.

"I—sorry, sir." Munk's distrust of anyone who did not work strictly to regulations was always liable to temporary amendment—there had been a time when Munk had thrown regulations to the wind, and with Dawlish saved a particularly nasty situation. Perhaps memory of that returned. "'Ell of a game, isn't it? The Inspector's come round, thank God."

"I'll echo that," said Dawlish soberly. "Do you want Mr. Farningham?"

"Ain't 'ad no instructions, sir." Munk remained quiet and unlike his usual self.

"Right—Bill, slip along to the flat, collect another gun—you know where they are—and then visit Chloë. Tell Sister Em it's positively a matter of life and death that she should speak before long, and make sure you see Chloë herself. Get an idea of what she's like—it's just possible she's foxing. Then ring the 'Shop' and tell them that Slim and Monty are the lousiest couple of blackguards I've ever heard of; they were supposed to follow Andy and Betty, but they've simply disappeared."

Bill shrugged. "In that shindy, can you blame them?"

Dawlish grinned. "Read between the lines," he said. "They may have reported to the 'Shop,' they might even have news of some kind, and certainly they should know what place Betty went to. If they're still alive, of course," he added gruffly.

Farningham was able to make his way from the cleared area as best he could, while Munk drove Dawlish to Scotland Yard. Piccadilly was closed from the Circus to Hyde Park Corner, and all traffic was being diverted. People thronged the streets—obviously news of the disaster had spread.

As they turned into the gates of the Yard, Munk ventured:

"You'll want to freshen up a bit, sir?" and Dawlish grinned at the hint and took it.

Five minutes later he emerged from the cloakroom feeling considerably fresher and fitter and made his way to Morely's office.

The A.C. had changed, and but for his bandaged hand and the gauntness of his face showed no signs of the affair in Piccadilly. With him were three men familiar to Dawlish, and standing nearest the window was the thickset figure of Sir Robert Knighton, Chief Constable. Not, Dawlish thought, an impressive C.C.

The Home Secretary, tall, willowy and grey-haired, was with the Defence Minister, a man of medium height dressed in almost dandified fashion. His rounded, benevolent features had lost much of their familiar geniality. As Dawlish entered, all three made an obvious effort to greet him naturally. Then Sir Archibald said dryly:

"Well, Dawlish, there seems little doubt you were right about their long-term preparations."

Dawlish nodded soberly. "Yes—and my visit and purchase made them aware of the possibility of a police raid, so the plan was put into operation. As far as I can tell there were no heavy parcels taken from Misslethwaites, which suggests there is a lot of cocaine and other stuff still there. It's being searched, is it?"

"Of course," said Knighton, a little stiffly. To his mind, Dawlish had been brought to answer questions, not to ask them.

"Their most important problem, was obviously to get the personnel safely away," Sir Archibald said. "Only three of the staff remained in the shop, and that suggests all of the others were concerned in the drug-distributing from Misslethwaites. The problem is—who was the leader?"

"There's a bigger one," said Dawlish quietly: "Where did the thirty-odd men go?"

"If they're in London, we'll find them," retorted Knighton sharply.

"How?" flashed Dawlish. "Not one was recognisable; they all wore gas-masks. But it's our main problem, gentlemen, and we haven't much time to lose." He spoke heavily, and the others stared, Morely among them.

"Why?" demanded the Minister.

"My dear sir," said Dawlish, "these people have been forced into the open since yesterday—*yesterday*—and they've adopted methods amounting to open warfare. *Unless* they were prepared to carry on with them they would not have started. What it is I don't know, but there's more than a crime-wave in the offing—there's a threat we can't properly appreciate. I'd say," he added, very softly and yet in a tone that carried an almost frightening grimness, "that I'm scared, gentlemen, scared to the marrow, in fact. You see—if there are thirty men there might be fifty. Or a hundred. Even more."

"What are you suggesting?" asked Knighton stiffly.

"I'm suggesting they're going on the rampage," snapped Dawlish. "I don't know how, I don't know where—but inside twenty-four hours we're going to see a minor hell in London, *unless* we find where they are."

The telephone rang sharply into the shocked silence. Morely lifted it, then looked at the Home Secretary.

"For you, Sir Arnold."

"Me? Right, thanks—"

Sir Arnold Clavering took the receiver, and his austere, aristocratic face was set, as if he were about to talk face to face with the man at the other end of the wire. Dawlish was watching him and saw his fingers tighten about the hand-instrument. The other heard him exclaim, and saw the expression on his face—it might have been dread, horror, consternation, disbelief: all four mingled.

"But—"

"There is no but," said the voice at the other end of the wire. It was suave and yet mellow, and although Clavering did not appreciate it, there was a tinge of sardonic humour in the full tone. "Unless, of course, you want a repetition of to-day's distressing occurrence, and I'm sure you would be opposed to that. Understand, please, that I am quite serious—"

Clavering's hand sagged, the ear-piece dropped several inches. Dawlish moved swiftly, took it, heard the suave voice, and interrupted in a fair imitation of Clavering's drawling, affected tone.

"Repeat *just* what you said, please."

"That," said the man at the other end of the wire, "suggests that you are going to be sensible. After all, you can do with a rest, Sir Arnold—" Dawlish heard the mocking, sardonic note, and was on tenter-hooks for what was coming—"and your immediate resignation will be understandable in view of to-day's disaster, *and* your poor health."

And Dawlish realised that the man at the other end of the wire was *demanding* the Home Secretary's resignation.

CHAPTER XXII

"RESIGN OR . . ."

It did not make sense.

Or at least it did not appear to, and Dawlish collected his wits as well as he could, hearing a repetition of the threat of another 'incident' like that of the afternoon. The casual voice at the other end of the wire did not sound flurried. It was cool and measured, and to Dawlish that of a man who not only knew what he wanted but believed he was going to get it. The calm effrontery of it did not seem important: the demand in itself was all that counted.

And the *reason* for it.

He saw that Morely was already speaking softly into another telephone, knew that the A.C. was having the call traced. And he answered, still in Clavering's affected voice:

"It—it is *quite* outrageous."

The other voice hardened.

"You've been told before—don't make the mistake this time of ignoring me. I shall expect the morning papers to report the resignation. Understand that!"

"But—"

"I've stayed quite long enough," said the speaker, and he laughed, a low-pitched mocking sound, before the line went dead.

Clavering was staring at Dawlish, his eyes narrowed and dull. Knighton and the Minister were on tenterhooks. Morely raised his voice:

"Quickly, please—where was that call from?"

"A telephone kiosk, sir, in Chelsea."

"Just where?"

"By the Town Hall, I think, sir. I'll confirm."

Morely pressed a bell while listening, and Trivett came in, hollow-eyed and yet in his movements alert enough.

"A man's just telephoned from the kiosk close to Chelsea Town Hall," snapped Morely. "Find him, and hurry. Don't waste a moment, Trivett . . . right, thanks." He banged down the receiver, having confirmation of the call-box's location from the operator. "It's absolutely vital, Trivett."

"At once, sir." Trivett disappeared as Dawlish replaced his own receiver and looked hard at Sir Arnold Clavering. In his mind a dozen questions were humming, and chief among them the *why* of this demand.

There was something which seemed hard to believe, and yet which had come so easily from the speaker's lips that there could be no object in doubting it.

"*You've been told before.*"

It was difficult to assess Clavering's attitude, and yet Dawlish knew that he had received a blow from which it was going to be difficult to recover. Only he and Dawlish knew what the demand had been, but the others were waiting: it would be impossible not to tell them.

Clavering cleared his throat, and as he spoke Dawlish felt admiration for a man who, in the past, he had viewed with mild toleration and at times almost contempt.

"Gentlemen, that was an outrageous message from someone I do not know, but who has been demanding—*demanding*—my resignation for some weeks past."

"Good God!" gasped Knighton blankly, and the Minister could only stare. Clavering lifted his hands, a helpless gesture.

"I've told you that much: I can do no more just now. I *must* discuss the matter with the Prime Minister before it goes further. Mr. Dawlish, I can rely on your discretion, of course?"

"You can," Dawlish said quietly. "But the ultimatum needs a quick answer, Sir Arnold."

"What ultimatum?" asked Knighton.

"My resignation or a similar outrage to that already suffered," said Clavering, and now that he had talked he seemed in firmer control of himself. "Until I have other instructions, Knighton, you will do nothing to interfere with present arrangements for apprehending the—the men concerned. Dawlish, of course, is right—it is likely to be crime on an unprecedented scale."

"You have a few hours," said Dawlish. "He said he expected to see the news in the morning's papers. There are a lot of things we can do in that time, Sir Arnold."

"Ye-es. Are you coming, Willison?"

The Minister nodded and groped somewhat blindly for his hat. Knighton went with them, and Morely looked at Dawlish, uncomprehending.

"What *does* it mean?"

Dawlish laughed, without humour.

"It's possible that they've been trying to blackmail Clavering into resigning; he's probably got a skeleton in the cupboard and he's likely to be telling the Prime Minister about it soon. But as far as this business is concerned, it means that they're using the crack-up of this morning to get Clavering jittery, to get rid of him, in short. As Home Secretary he controls so much,

Morely—you and Knighton, for a start. With a Home Secretary who was more easily amenable to—er—suggestions, that might be important. Who'd take his place?"

Morely stared. "That's fantastic—"

"It all is. I suppose Garner's the most likely man, and Devoe is a close second." Dawlish saw mind-pictures of two other Cabinet Ministers, each of whom had been 'tipped' during the last Cabinet reshuffle as Clavering's likely successor. "I'll see whether I can get anything about them—but like most of the other things it's an aside; it's not the main issue. The main issue once looked like being drugs. I wonder if it is?"

"Can't the Farrimond woman talk?" snapped Morely.

"I don't know. Farningham's trying to find out, but it might be an idea if one of the Harley Street men examined her. I doubt if she'll know much; if she did she wouldn't be alive. They must know where she is. And we must know where they are, Morely; until we've located them we can't get away with a thing. And we haven't a line, unless Slim and Monty found one."

"Who?"

"Friends of mine," said Dawlish, and would not elaborate. "There's just a chance," he added, "that the post-mortem on the man who died at de Mond Mansions might help. Did you know him, by the way?"

Morely started. "Lord, I'd forgotten. Yes, he's been through our hands a dozen times, usually on trivial offences. A Dr. Arthur Sloane—drink and drugs slowly killed a decent suburban practice; the last we'd heard of him he was in lodgings in Bethnal Green, practising unofficially. He was struck off the register for unprofessional conduct twelve years ago. A wreck of a man, Dawlish."

"He looked it, yes. How long since you've had him here?"

"Oh—three years or more. We'd lost trace of him for eighteen months."

They were both silent for a few moments. Then wearily, Morely held his head in his hands for a moment, more dejected than Dawlish had ever seen him. "Sorry," he said stiffly. "But all this—it just doesn't make sense. I feel as if I'm sitting on a volcano."

"Precisely what I've been feeling since yesterday afternoon," said Dawlish. "No Morrell—Chloë right out with some blasted drug—Lady Betty missing again, Misslethwaites destroying a hundred years' reputation—by the way, the board of Misslethwaites. You're checking up?"

"Of course. There are three directors, two of them just names—Mortimer Grayson and Lord Ankrett—and the managing-director is a son-in-law of the last Misslethwaite, a man named Adams."

Dawlish said slowly: "Adams—*Adams?*"

He shouted the name the second time, and Morely stared at him.

"Yes, does the name mean anything to you?"

"Oh, my Lord!" exclaimed Dawlish, "there's certainly no sense in this. *Adams!* Morely, there's a Colonel Robert Adams living in de Mond Mansions. Be discreet and find if he's any relative of the Misslethwaite gentleman."

"My dear man, the name's not unusual."

"Nor as common as you might think," Dawlish insisted.

"Adams has been to the Manchester branch of the firm—I 'phoned the office. Yes," Morely added, as Dawlish started to speak, "I've also told the Manchester police to have him followed, and the four branches of the firm in Great Britain are being closely watched. But there's going to be no precipitate action this time, Dawlish—we're not risking another horror like to-day's."

"I'm not blaming you for that," said Dawlish. "But it isn't in your hands, old man. If the powers-that-be see fit not to let

Clavering resign, we'll get one. And as it's bound to be a matter of considerable importance, we're not likely to know what Clavering's skeleton is."

"You're certainly associating yourself with us," said Morely dryly.

"At your invitation," grinned Dawlish. "Look—let's go back to the start—" He was standing in front of the empty fireplace, his hands deep in his pockets, his face revealing his concentration: "Drugs—and the thing that worried you was drugs in high places. The Black Out Club was suggested and the Chloë-Morrell angle suggests there might be something in it. There was also the Night Templar. Why suspect?"

Morely frowned. "Known distributors—people who used to handle the stuff—were frequenters."

"They haven't been raided?"

"No."

"It might be an idea if you went through them to-night," said Dawlish, then hesitated. "Or before to-night—before the crowds get there and real damage can be caused. If there's a rendezvous at either of them, it should show some results."

"Yes . . . Two days ago I would have said we'd nothing to raid them on, but now—" Morely hesitated. "Do you want to be on the spot?"

"No. But if I dare suggest it—it *might* create a shindy like this afternoon's, so if you have plenty of men about, it might help."

"I'll have a look at them," Morely promised. He eyed Dawlish keenly. "What will you be doing?"

"I don't know—yet." Dawlish hesitated. "There's one connection, as far as I can see, between this business with Clavering and the drugs affair. A man at the Foreign Office and another at the Home Office—or was it Admiralty?"

"Admiralty," said Morely quietly.

"Hmm. Well, they're known drug-addicts. There might be a lot of people who take the stuff but aren't known."

"What are you driving at, Dawlish?"

"I'm not really sure myself," said Dawlish slowly. "But the Home Secretary *was* virtually ordered to resign while in the office of the Assistant Commissioner of Scotland Yard. They *are* big."

"Whatever you're thinking, you should pass on," said Morely sharply.

"Oh, no," said Dawlish. "I pass on facts and keep my fancies to myself. In this particular case, very much to myself. See about that Adams angle, will you?"

He lifted a hand and moved towards the door. Morely started to protest, then realised that it was useless. The A.C. was more perturbed than he liked to admit. He was out of his depth, he was afraid of what might happen, yet he had not the slightest idea what it might be. Dawlish, with his uncanny habit of getting to the heart of the matter, might guess.

"Impossible!" snorted Morely, and felt better.

Half an hour later, he had three reports on his desk. The first claimed that as far as was known Mr. Charles Mullinger Adams had no male relatives, and he smiled a little grimly at the failure of one long shot of Dawlish's. There was little to smile at in the rest of that report, for Charles Mullinger Adams had left Manchester early that afternoon, and had not been seen since.

"He could be on the way to London," Morely thought, aloud. "I'll have St. Pancras watched." He gave the necessary instructions by telephone, and took the second report from his desk. He read it, scowling. It was a house-memo, stating that the necessary precautions had been taken by the police of Manchester, Glasgow, Birmingham and Sheffield to watch the premises of

Misslethwaites, gold and silversmiths, in accordance with the Scotland Yard and Home Office request.

Morely found his mind side-tracking. *Why* did these people want Clavering removed from office?

He pushed the thought aside, and looked at the third report. It comprised the total list of casualties in the battle of the Arcade. There were, so far, twenty-four deaths, thirty-three seriously injured, and over a hundred casualties in need of medical attention. A frightening list—a frightening ruthlessness. And there were virtually no contacts, unless Chloë Farrimond was one—and Chloë, according to a specialist who had 'phoned him earlier, was suffering from shock as well as the results of an unknown—or at least unrecognised—poison.

Too big, Dawlish had said.

Morely felt that he was right—the whole affair was too big; too alarming. But what was it, what did it mean, what was likely to happen?

The same question was in Dawlish's mind as he walked along Whitehall towards Trafalgar Square, and took the longer route to Piccadilly and thus Brook Street. He reached his flat, went warily upstairs, and wondered whether Farningham had been lucky in finding the two men from the 'Shop' or any trace of them.

The 'Shop' had on its books several ex-Yard men who were also interested in physical training, and the manager would not have sent anyone untrained in shadowing to watch Cunningham and Betty. Reliable men should have sent word, unless the Piccadilly disaster had disabled them.

He unlocked the door of his flat, flung it open, hesitated and, when he felt reasonably sure there was no one inside, went through. And as he went he stopped short, and his stomach heaved.

For two men were lying on the carpet, side by side—
Hefty-looking men, quite dead.

As he stared, he knew they were the men who had followed Lady Betty as her bodyguard. They had been killed by knife-cuts in the throat—as horribly as Jeffery, Sir Louis Morrell's secretary.

CHAPTER XXIII

A SECOND MEETING

At the time that Dawlish was discovering the murder of his assistants, there were five people in the study at the Wimbledon house. Larramy was standing, the other four sitting. Number Four, who so rarely appeared at the meetings, was in Larramy's chair, and facing his three colleagues. Larramy himself looked even paler than when Dawlish had seen him, and his eyes were those of a fanatic.

"It's suicide, I tell you. You can't go on like this! If I'd known—"

"You do precisely what you are told to do," said Number Four. Like One and Two he was bearded—and his beard was jet-black, neatly trimmed and yet heavy enough to disguise the half of his face completely. He had a sharp, incisive voice, and Dawlish would have recognised the timbre as that of the man who had talked to Clavering. "You have had control of a part of our organisation, Larramy, and up to a point you have done well. In the present emergency you are showing yourself in a less favourable light. Dawlish has escaped completely; you were not responsible for Sloane's death; you had made no preparations—"

"I told Muller to shoot."

"The report is that Muller did shoot, and missed."

"He was driving at the same time, you can't expect miracles!" snarled Larramy. "I want to know more about it, that Piccadilly show in particular."

"It's nothing to do with you," snapped Four.

"I know Misslethwaites was one of our clearing-houses."

"The affair there was arranged by us," said Four more calmly, "but it remains none of your business. As far as I can discover all you have done that is satisfactory is to get the Lorne woman, and that was half-done for you; two men who were shadowing her were removed."

Larramy started. "Who—?"

"It was arranged," said Four. "Now, Larramy, listen. This house is reasonably safe, although if Sloane had lived it would not be; he would have talked. There are several of your men who might talk, and in consequence no one of them is to leave here until I give permission. Is that understood?"

"I—" Larramy, who had reckoned he was the equal of any man, was frightened, and it was not hard to see that. "I'm telling you you can't get away with this."

"We have and we will. Listen, Larramy, we have three hundred men waiting for the moment we say go."

"Three *hundred!*"

"And more if they're needed," said the man with the black beard. Behind his thick-lensed glasses his eyes were sharp and angry, but there was a variety of reasons why they should not antagonise Abraham Larramy just then. "We shall proceed for a week, or a little more, Larramy, and among the things we have to do is hold-up deliveries of foods from Southampton and Liverpool. I'm giving you fifty men, and you will handle the Southampton end."

"But how?"

"Don't act like a schoolboy!" snarled Four. "You'll have all information about road and railway shipments. Larramy, you've taken an easy twenty thousand pounds as your share of the proceeds—or haven't you kept a record?"

Larramy straightened up, and even essayed a smile.

"That's right, twenty-one thousand."

"You will have that doubled in a week," said Four, "if you carry out instructions. They're simple enough."

"Yeah," said Larramy, and uninvited he sat down on the arm of a chair. "But how'm I to work this if no one's to go out of the house?"

"That didn't include you—tell the others what you like, but make sure no one goes out. Any of your people who are out now can come in, but they're to stop."

"Why?"

"I've told you—we don't want this place located. When the time comes we can get somewhere else."

"Okay," said Abraham Larramy, and he grinned. "The twenty thousand comes my way right now, I reckon."

"You'll get half now, and half when it's over. And Larramy, it was necessary to get rid of Lancelot Grey, I admit, but you should have blamed the police for the accident. Jonathan has been talking, and he is not well-disposed towards you. I'm warning you to be careful if you should meet him again. I don't want trouble from inside."

"You don't have to worry about Grey," said Larramy, and he swaggered from the arm of the chair. "Anything else, gentlemen?"

"The payment and further instructions will reach you before the night's out," said Four. "Work immediately, and don't make mistakes."

"Give me the men, I'll do your work for you."

"Excellent," said One, speaking smoothly for the first time. "All righ, Larramy, we are leaving immediately."

Larramy nodded. One stepped towards the door after picking up his hat and coat. The others were just behind him as he opened it—and opening it, he heard a rustle of satin. Ma Flannigan's pock-marked face was staring expressionlessly at One, who started back.

The woman tossed her head, sneered, and marched away. The four Members repressed their comments, and went downstairs to the closed car. While in the study Abraham Larramy was wondering how long he dare wait before he cleaned up and disappeared. There were times when things grew too hot, and he believed such a time was at hand.

CHAPTER XXIV

FACTS, NOT FANCIES

Patrick Dawlish stood for some seconds in the doorway of the room. Then he stepped over the two bodies to the telephone and called Morely.

"Dawlish again," he said heavily. "You'll recall my talk of Slim and Monty. They were two ex-Yard men I had from Tony's Gymnasium—you know it, of course."

"Yes. What about them?"

"Lured to my flat," said Dawlish, "and there murdered in precisely the same way as Jeffery. If you've forgotten Jeffery, he was Morrell's secretary. Clever, isn't it?" Morely said something but Dawlish went on as though unaware of an interruption. "I *could* have committed the Staines murder, you know, and then hopped back to the Station for the cab and arrived at River Lodge with an alibi all nicely set. Likewise I could have killed these poor beggars myself; it's the same trade mark."

"Stop drivelling," said Morely. "How long have the men been dead?"

"Not long, I'd say. Just a moment—" Dawlish stooped down, and touched the outflung arm of the man nearer him. "Quite warm; probably they were alive fifteen minutes ago. Their instructions were to follow Lady Betty, and almost certainly they obeyed them. She was in the Arcade a short while before the mess there. I'm not yet sure whether this is an awful warning to me not to meddle, or whether they're deliberately trying to frame me. Any ideas?"

"I'll send Munk over. I can't spare anyone else for an hour or two. He'll take your instructions."

"Thanks. Meanwhile, try to find from the local boys if a car was seen outside here in the recent past, will you? And did you get that specialist's report on Chloë?"

"Yes—it's quite genuine."

"Hmm. If only we knew what Chloë knows. No trace of any of the others, I take it. . . ? No. Adams?"

"The Misslethwaite man is 'Charles Mullinger' and he isn't known to have a male relative."

"Not helpful. Grayson and Ankrett?"

"They're on the way to London," said Morely, "with some local men. Ankrett isn't pleased at being told to come. He doesn't appear to take his job as a director of Misslethwaites very seriously. Grayson, I'm told, thinks it a bore—he's the type."

"Ye-es." Dawlish knew Lord Ankrett by sight and reputation. He was a peer on the wrong side of middle-age, very conscious of his position and, being a die-hard of die-hards, convinced that the country was going to rack and ruin. Mortimer Grayson, on the other hand, was a different type—suave, well-mannered; Eton and Balliol; but a man-about-town in—Dawlish privately considered—the worst sense of the word. A dandy with a reputation for style not far below Morrell's, he spent four months of the year on the Riviera, and the rest in England. As directors of Misslethwaites both men were purely decorative; the man who mattered there was Charles Mullinger Adams.

"What of your Adams?" he asked.

"He's on his way to London, I hope," said Morely.

"Like that, is it. Well now, Garner and Devoe—you still don't know who is most likely to step into Clavering's shoes?"

"I don't know that anyone will."

"Oh yes, they will," said Dawlish with confidence, "He's going to resign, and the statement to that effect will be in the morning papers, I'll bet my last shilling on that. So it's either Garner or Devoe."

"I'm not a political prophet," said Morely wearily. "I don't see that it makes a great deal of difference."

"No ... You might try discreetly to pry into their private lives, old man. After all, the Home Secretary is a whale of a fellow, and these days, what with one thing and another we can't call our lives our own. Or can we?"

Morely knew the big man well enough to realise that Dawlish covered many things of importance with that almost asinine manner.

"I'll inquire where I can," he said cautiously.

"Do, there's a good fellow. Facts, not fancies, mind you. Anything from Misslethwaites yet?"

Morely drew a deep breath. "The cellars are filled with cocaine and heroin, Dawlish; we've found our source of supply. The stuff has been coming into the country consigned to Misslethwaites, who've such a reputation that their declared imports have been accepted with only a cursory examination by the Customs people." The A.C. laughed, unexpectedly. "Yesterday morning I would have been sitting down and congratulating myself about the find, but now—why *do* you always land us in for something more than we expect, Dawlish?"

"Me?" Dawlish protested. "Don't blame me, blame those brushes. They got lost and started this trouble—but it must have been ripe for starting anyhow. No word about Grey or Doc Sloane?"

"No trace at all yet, but there's been little time."

"There remains little time," said Dawlish.

"Dawlish, what have you got on your mind?"

"Look, old son," Dawlish said, "If they can kick Clavering out of office, there's no limit to what they can manage. We've uncovered their drug base, or one of them, but we haven't the slightest reason in the world for thinking that's all they're handling. However, fancies aren't facts, and I want facts. Don't we all?"

"I'll send Munk over at once," said Morely sharply, and rang off.

Dawlish replaced the receiver, lit a cigarette and then brought a blanket from the spare bedroom and put it gently over the bodies of Slim and Monty. He had seen them only for a few minutes, and yet in a way they had died for him. It was not a pleasant thought, and he pushed it aside for the time being. He was actually dialling Farningham's number when Bill, who had a key of the flat, came in. He looked dishevelled and tired, but not particularly alarmed. He saw the bundles on the floor, and frowned at Dawlish.

"What's this? And I'm thirsty."

"Beer in the cabinet," said Dawlish. "We'll drink it in the other room." He explained as he carried two bottles into the small dining-room, and perched on the corner of the table. "Altogether a nasty business. Had they reported to the 'Shop'?"

"No—no word."

"Hmm. Nothing of Betty?"

"No." Farningham lowered his beer thoughtfully, and his tongue ran along his lips. "I'm not liking it a bit, Pat. Do you think Andy's story was wholly genuine?"

"You've wondered about Andy, have you?"

"Damn it, I've had to. No man in his senses would have sent that stuff to Millie's, for instance."

"No . . . Is a man in love in full possession of his senses?" asked Dawlish gently. "It's a moot point. Anyhow, I don't know whether Andy is putting anything across us, but I'm prepared to wager that Betty's all right. And she's gone. We have also to consider the fact that Slim and Monty were brought here and murdered, in the flat. Cool work; the kind of work the Greys might have done, or one Grey since Lancelot is dead. Bill—" Dawlish put his hand into his breast pocket, drew out a pencil and then a small diary. He opened the diary and as he talked, slowly but clearly, he was scribbling. "Bill, there are two distinct shows running side by side. Quite obviously the brushes hold a secret concerning personnel. The desperate effort to retrieve them suggests that the leader, or a leader, of this racket could be betrayed by the brushes."

Farningham scowled.

"Why so obvious?"

Dawlish considered. "Well, here is a drug-racket running very smoothly, and judging from the quantities involved probably showing a profit of some tens of thousands a month. Other things have been prepared, and waiting for the kick-off, but the only reason why a big show like the drugs should be jeopardised is the possibility—I say possibility, Bill—that the leader might be found. The start of major operations really coincided with the loss of the brushes, there's no doubt of that."

"Involved," said Farningham judiciously, and he took a note which Dawlish pushed across the table towards him. "I wouldn't call it proved, old man, not by a long chalk. And I think—" he broke off, and then spoke again in the same tone, although his thoughts as voiced added nothing to the general knowledge.

Only the expression in his eyes showed what he was feeling, for Dawlish had written:

Flat occupied. Stand by.
Look surprised.

"You think all wrong," said Dawlish, and he sounded testy. Speaking, he glance towards the closed door, and he saw the handle turning slowly. From the first, from the moment he had realised that the two men had been killed inside the flat, he had realised the probability that others were present, and he particularly wanted to create the impression that he had no such idea. "Once we find those brushes, Bill, we should get places."

And then the door opened abruptly, and he saw Jonathan Grey standing there, pale-faced and as vague-looking as when he had first appeared in Dawlish's ken, except that he now carried an automatic which was fitted with a silencer. His lips were compressed tightly and there was venom in the slate-grey eyes.

Farningham stepped back a pace, and made a sharp movement towards his pocket. The gun in Grey's hand moved up sharply as he snapped:

"Keep still. Dawlish, I haven't come for a long visit. I've heard enough, and I've heard that you don't know anything of importance, but you're right about those brushes. They—" he stopped, and his tongue poked out and darted along his lips. "Never mind about that now. You've been ineffective most of the time, but you killed my brother."

Dawlish said, as though with an effort:

"Don't be a fool! Your own men—"

"If you had stayed away from Lister Street there would have been no trouble. I was fond of my brother, Dawlish, I'm killing you because of him, not for any other reason. I've had those instructions but I don't give a damn about instructions; before I'm through I'll shoot every man who took any part in Lance's murder. Understand?"

"You don't seem to stop at murder yourself," Dawlish said, and his breathing was sharp and quick, his eyes roved about the room as if seeking some means of escape. "Doesn't it occur to you that he got what was coming to him? As did Sloane? I—"

"Sloane was a drunken sot, he was useful only because he could save us from calling-in outside medical help." Grey shrugged. "But I'm wasting time." He put his left hand into his pocket, and brought out a small note-pad, and a pencil. He tossed them to the table, where they stopped after the pencil rolled against the edge of the pad. "Write to my dictation, Dawlish."

The gun moved, and Dawlish picked up the pencil slowly. Farningham, helpless and more afraid than he liked, wondered whether Dawlish had anything prepared, wondered whether he had known for long that Grey was in the flat.

"Write this:

Dear Lady Betty,

If you are advised by me you will carry out the suggestions of the bearer of this note. I can see no object at all in your refusing, it will cause both trouble and perhaps disaster on a scale greater than that which you saw this afternoon. Andy, I can as sure you, is quite safe and well—any objections which you raise might well make it even more difficult and dangerous for him. Believe me, I have written this only after much consideration, and, please, believe me to be, yours most sincerely, Patrick Dawlish.

Dawlish felt a moment of elation, for he could have had no better proof that over some matter of importance, Lady Betty was proving awkward.

Grey tossed an envelope.

"Write her name on that."

"What's the address?" asked Dawlish as he started to write, and Farningham's eyes narrowed. Dawlish hardly believed it possible to get any result; the effort was as long a shot as he had ever made. He might not have made it but for the feeling that Grey was thinking of something else even while he dictated.

"Clunes, Common Road, Wimble—" Grey stopped, lifted his head sharply, and snapped: "You think you're clever, Dawlish! If I'd told you it all it wouldn't have helped you."

And then Dawlish tossed a little glass phial into his face.

He did it so quickly that Farningham was taken by surprise, while Dawlish just bent his knees, lowering his height by a full six inches. A bullet from Grey's automatic snapped out, hummed over Dawlish's head and struck against the wall—at the same second as the glass phial broke. Grey gasped—and gasping drew in the cloud of ammonia gas which escaped, and as he reeled Dawlish leapt forward and struck the gun out of his hand.

"Open the window, Bill." He shouted the order as he felt the first bite of the gas himself, and as Grey reached the floor, clawing at his face.

Farningham flung the window open while Dawlish threw the door wide. A cool draught of air passed through, he coughed a little as the gas bit at his throat, and there were tears in his eyes as well as Farningham's. But Grey was out of action, *and Dawlish had Lady Betty's address.*

He said hoarsely: "Lucky I took those things from Lancelot, Bill—I'd a feeling they'd come in useful. Run through his pockets. I want to 'phone Morely again. Facts, this time, not fancies!"

And he laughed—but the laugh was not a thing of humour.

CHAPTER XXV

CLUNES, COMMON ROAD

"Yes," said Morely tensely. "Yes . . . of course I understand that. But Dawlish, are you sure?"

"If you get moving now I'll guarantee you'll find her at the house," said Dawlish. "And if you move too slowly, I'll guarantee you'll find her dead. How quickly do you think it can be managed?"

"Twenty minutes."

"Make it fifteen or less! And then get reinforcements. Have the place so locked up that no one can escape, but for the love of Mike don't let anyone going in suspect that you're about. Anyone coming out ought to get well away from the house first."

"Thanks for the advice," said Morely dryly. "What are you doing?"

"I'm going in, I hope," said Dawlish. "You might warn the Wimbledon people that a tall, handsome, fair-haired man will be going in, and should be treated with veneration." He grinned into the telephone. "I'm taking Farningham with me, although he doesn't realise it yet and probably won't appreciate it. Seriously—if we can get inside, we might stop more tragedy. It's a chance, anyhow. And if they lock themselves in like they did at the Arcade there'll be hell to pay. Once I'm inside, I'd suggest that the roads are blocked, and the nearby houses evacuated."

He replaced the receiver as Farningham looked up from Grey's writhing body. The man was conscious and moaning. As Dawlish knew only too well the pain of the ammonia gas was almost unbearable, and Grey was still clawing at his streaming eyes.

Farningham had emptied Grey's pocket's and now passed over several papers.

Dawlish took two of the sheets and saw that they were covered with figures which, to him, were nothing but an array of hieroglyphics. He scowled, and was still scowling when there were heavy footsteps on the stairs, followed by a knock on the outer door.

"Munk," said Dawlish. "And in nice time, thanks be. Bill, Morely's having a cordon flung round this place Clunes, but delaying action until you and I have tried to get in. That is, if you're game to make it. We mightn't get out."

Farningham frowned, his pugnacious face worried, and he pushed a hand through his untidy hair.

"I wish I'd had time for a word with Di."

"I know," said Dawlish quietly. "Bill, I'll make it myself. You stand by."

"Fiddlesticks." Farningham grinned. "I couldn't trust you on your own, anyhow." He broke off as the knocking came again on the door, this time more heavily. "Could Munk come in?"

Dawlish smiled. "Thanks, old man. *Enter, sergeant!*" His bellow brought Munk straight in, two C.I.D. men behind him. Dawlish put a hand on his shoulder, sober and confidential.

"Munk, this is serious. The two men you've been told about are under that blanket. There's another cove in the other room—you can hear him moaning—who wants watching closer than anything you've ever watched in your life. The other Grey."

Munk's eyes widened: admiration gleamed in them.

"I'll see to '*im*—"

"Probably he didn't come alone. Are you armed?"

"Yes. Special permission."

"Fine. Stand by the window as I go downstairs, and if I'm followed and there looks like being trouble, pick the man or men off. If you've any doubts about it, remember the Arcade. Got all that?"

"Ye-es," said Munk, but now he looked startled. "Sir Archibald didn't say—"

"He put you under my orders. I mustn't be followed, Munk, and for the time being I want to stay alive—for the good of the community. Got all that now?"

"Yes, sir." The moustaches quivered; Munk was beginning to feel indignant, and in such a mood he was at his efficient best.

"Good. Then hand these papers—" Dawlish passed over the sheets covered with figures to the sergeant—"to Sir Archibald personally. My compliments, and suggest that they go to the Cypher Department at once. And also, Mr. Farningham's compliments and if there should be any delay in our return, will he get in touch with Miss Diana Lefroy in person, and explain what happened?"

Munk stared, as if to understand just why Dawlish had said that. Indignation disappeared, and he spoke quietly, appreciatively.

"Yes, sir, I'll see to it all. Good luck, sir."

"Thanks," said Dawlish. "We'll go, Bill—no, a moment."

He went to the cocktail cabinet, took his flask from his hip pocket, and replenished it. There was an odd smile on his lips. He replaced the stopper and then, from a drawer revealed by the pressing of a concealed button, took a small packet of .32 ammunition. He slipped it into his pocket, and deliberately winked at Munk. "Strictly between ourselves, sergeant!"

Munk said soberly: "I hope you won't need 'em, sir," and Dawlish nodded agreement as he followed Farningham downstairs.

Farningham's Rover, with new tyres, was standing outside; its outlines blurred by the gathering dusk. He opened the door of the driving seat, and as he pressed the self-starter a man moved from the other side of the road.

And another, from the same side but further along.

"May Munk be quick," said Dawlish, and glanced towards the end of Brook Street. There was no one else in sight, a rare thing. "I—"

He did not hear the report, for the gun was silenced: but he saw the stab of blue flame that seemed to spring from the hand of the nearer man, and heard the *whang!* of the bullet against and through the nearside back wing. He ducked, the car jolted forward—and then from the window came two loud reports: Munk had seen the attack and was in action.

There was a scream—

The man opposite the Rover dropped, his gun clattering, and the man farther along stayed put but fired twice. A bullet drilled a small neat hole through the windscreen, but as it did so Munk fired again—and Munk knew how to use a Webley. Dawlish saw the second man fall as Farningham steadied the wheel and scorched to the end of Brook Street. He took the corner sharply, then swung his wheel to the right, avoiding an oncoming Rolls by a hair's breadth. The passenger in the Rolls leaned forward sharply—and Dawlish saw the pale, drawn face of Sir Arnold Clavering.

"Funny thing, coincidence," he said. "Slow down, we don't want that peeler sending a call for us."

Farningham obeyed as a policeman who had seen what seemed a piece of criminal driving hurried across Piccadilly. As he approached, fully prepared to be righteously angry, Dawlish took out the pass from Morely. As before, it worked a miracle.

"Thanks." Dawlish flashed a smile. "Right, Bill—Clunes, first stop."

"Do you happen to know where it is?"

"I know where Common Road is," said Dawlish. "We'll just make it before it gets too dark."

Farningham grunted. "That's fine. And when we've made it, do we just go up to the front door or fly through one of the windows?"

Dawlish chuckled. "The front door, old man, it's far more comfortable. Dawlish and Farningham, Incorporated, Private Sleuths—hungering for all the glory."

Victoria—Chelsea—Fulham—Putney—left and over the bridge—Putney Hill—

"Common Road," said Dawlish. "Bear left and keep straight on, old man." Glancing to the right, he saw three cars drawn up at the kerb—and rightly suspected they were police cars. Trivett had been busy: the Wimbledon police had flung a cordon about Clunes, a cordon which would be closed tight when Dawlish and Farningham were inside.

When? Or if?

Dawlish pushed the question aside. It was useless to work on any other assumption than a successful entry. It was a gamble, but the circumstances demanded one—and he could say with honesty that nothing he suspected had been withheld from the police. If the worst came to the worst and this was the end for him, Morely could carry on. The loss of Dawlish and Farningham would not be of great moment to anyone.

Except Diana, where Bill was concerned.

He said: "Time to change your mind, old man."

"Nothing doing."

"Right. Slow down, there's a postman." Farningham obeyed and Dawlish opened the window, to ask the postman to direct them to Clunes. As he did so a burly man walked slowly past, and Dawlish knew that the police, on foot as well were comfortingly close at hand.

"Five or six houses along, sir, you can't miss it: there's a big 'edge."

"Thanks." Dawlish smiled. "Right, Bill."

The thick yew hedge around the house of Abraham Larramy was plain enough, even in the increasing gloom. The squat outlines of the house, built on Georgian lines, showed against the darkening sky. Behind some bushes on the Common opposite, Dawlish saw two men. The sight gave added comfort.

"The gate's open," Farningham said. "Straight in?"

"Yes—and scorch."

"Right." Farningham swung the wheel and, once on the short carriage drive, trod heavily on the accelerator. There was a screech of tyres on gravel and then a squealing of brakes as he reached the front door. The car jolted to a standstill, and Dawlish pushed open the door and leapt up the steps, with Farningham only a yard behind him. Both men were breathing hard, for there were so many things they might expect—a burst of machine-gun fire among them.

But the house was silent.

Dawlish rang the old-fashioned bell-pull and the ringing clanged inside the hall, deep and cavernous. For good measure he banged heavily on the iron knocker—but all the time he kept his right hand in his pocket. Farningham did likewise.

"Possibly no one at home?" said Farningham, almost hopefully.

"They'd hardly leave Betty here alone—and Grey didn't lie, I'll swear to that. Bill, if we come a cropper here and Morely finds out we're taking a chance on our own, we won't be popular at the Yard in future."

Farningham stared, as Dawlish grimaced at him, then caught on, and said aggrievedly:

"I told you it was a damned silly idea!"

Quite abruptly, and without a sound, the front door opened. The man in the hall was the thin-lipped, vicious-faced Kramm— the chauffeur who had talked with Lady Betty. His lips were parted in what passed for a smile, while the gun in his hand did not waver.

"It was more than silly, you poor punk! Get your hands out of those pockets—"

Dawlish began: "I—"

"And put them above your heads," said a voice from behind him. It was a throaty voice, and it held an ominous note. Dawlish turned his head, and saw a thick-set man, also holding a gun, standing at the foot of the steps. "Look snappy!"

Dawlish obeyed, and Farningham followed suit: anything else was suicidal. With their hands above their heads they stepped into the large, frowsty-looking hall of Clunes, and the thick-set gunman followed them. With Kramm keeping them covered from the front, Schuster ran through their pockets, taking out their guns—and from Dawlish the spare ammunition.

"You won't need this," he sneered. "Upstairs, and don't try the funny stuff. These bullets are for real."

Dawlish started forward. Farningham, knowing this was according to plan yet feeling helpless and very nearly hopeless, followed him. And as the door closed, the watchers opposite signalled to the carloads of police waiting farther along.

From all sides, without fuss of ostentation, the police closed in on Clunes; while other officers began to call on the residents of the nearer houses, advising them to evacuate without saying why.

To questions, they answered: "Home Office orders, sir," or "Madam," as the case might be; and they met with surprisingly little opposition. And while they carried on, and while the cordon of local men closed in, Morely, Trivett, and a dozen picked men from the Yard were racing to the scene and a detachment of troops was being moved up in support.

Each man had a gas-mask.

For a quarter of a mile radius, the traffic was stopped or diverted and the roads barricaded.

Darkness had almost fallen when Morely and Trivett reached the party of Wimbledon police near the house.

"Nothing developed?" Morely asked the local Superintendent.

"No, sir."

But the words were hardly out of his mouth when from an upstairs window of the house there came a blinding flash of white light—and the crash of breaking window. For a split-second the outline of the house was clearly visible in the billow of white smoke that followed the flash. Then darkness, with only a dull glow from the room with the broken window to relieve it.

Darkness, and a silence which seemed more ominous because it was the last thing they expected.

CHAPTER XXVI

LIGHT IN THE DARKNESS

"Absolutely a cinch, boss." Kramm was grinning as he stood in front of Larramy, at the table used so often by members of that mysterious association which controlled the big racketeer. "The musical box by the door worked a treat: the mike put what they said right over. They've come on their own, and they're wishing they hadn't."

Larramy grunted. "All right, Kramm. Stay here for a while, and at the first sign of a trick, use your gat. Send them in."

In a few seconds Dawlish and Farningham entered, their hands still above their heads, and Schuster behind them with his gun. Dawlish saw the pallid face and the feverish bright eyes of the man he had seen only once before, at Chloë's flat.

Larramy's lips twisted in a sneer.

"You look pretty, Dawlish—you and your boy friend. You can put your hands down, but keep them in sight."

Dawlish drawled: "Nice of you. But be warned—we are not alone, little man."

"Don't lie!" snarled Larramy. "There's a microphone at the front door; all that's said there comes through!"

Dawlish's mouth dropped.

"Good God—!"

"You can save your prayers," sneered Larramy. "How'd you make this place?"

Dawlish made what appeared to be a considerable effort, and even found a smile. "Your friend Grey came, and he's not so brilliant. He dictated a letter, and when it was finished I dropped one of his brother's ammonia phials nearby—it worked this time, too. Grey cracked."

Larramy swore. "I always told them those swine were yellow-bellied, I—"—he recovered himself—"All right. Grey gave you this address. What else?"

"There were a couple of men watching. I handled them."

"And that made you feel mighty proud of yourself," sneered Larramy. "What have you got for a mind, Dawlish? How did you expect to get through here?"

Dawlish shrugged: "Grey said there were only two people here as well as Lady Betty."

"He wasn't such a fool as I thought," said Larramy, and he grinned. "You're all washed up, Dawlish, and maybe you'll like to know that I'm going off right now for a little job that will make Morely and his precious fools sit up. *Right* now, Dawlish, when I've finished with you." He stood up, still grinning. "Open the door, Kramm. Dawlish, we're going to see that dame, and you're going to tell her what that letter told you to. Follow?"

Farningham snapped: "Why the Devil should we, if—"

Larramy swung round.

"You'll get yours, but the dame'll get off easier if she does what I say; if she doesn't—remember what Lancelot Grey suggested? It seemed a bum idea at the time, but it looks good now. Tell her to obey orders—got it?"

"What are the orders?" asked Dawlish.

"You'd like to know!" Larramy slipped a gun from a shoulder-holster. "Get upstairs—Schuster, you lead. Kramm, come up behind. No side-tricks, Dawlish."

Farningham was wondering whether Dawlish had counted too much on his luck, and whether the pale-faced man's preparedness would be too foolproof.

Larramy was feeling fully satisfied for the first time since his interview with the Members. They had jolted his self-conceit, and the complete humiliation of Dawlish restored it.

Dawlish was wondering when the right moment would come to pull his trick; he had just one, and if it failed—

He shrugged, for there was little use in contemplating the hereafter. At least he would see Betty, and already it seemed reasonably certain that she was safe enough so far. There was one question concerning her which he found it hard to answer even in theory.

What could Larramy want from her?

The letter which Grey had dictated had made it plain that they were demanding something and that she was refusing to give it. Information, thought Dawlish. But when he wondered *what* information, he was stymied. What could she know?

He doubted whether it concerned Andy Cunningham: the mention of Andy in the dictated letter had obviously been an attempt at coercing her with the threat of trouble for Andy.

Did she know anything?

He frowned. The older Grey had kidnapped her, but that had been only as a means of persuading Cunningham to give up the silver brushes. At that time, then, it had not been suspected that she had information or that she could do something. Which suggested that from the time she had been rescued to the time of the outrage in the Arcade, she had learned something which had made her a vital factor in the affair as far as Pale-face was concerned.

They reached the second landing of the house, a small, unfurnished landing with a strip of frayed carpet leading along the two passages, which went right and left. Dawlish's lips twisted wryly when he realised where he was, that for the moment he had been lost completely in thought of Betty and other problems. Schuster and Kramm, their guns ostentatiously in evidence, might be calculated to stop him thinking of that, but they had failed. Dawlish was fond of admitting that he had a one-track mind . . .

Farningham's face was set; Dawlish's smile disappeared when he thought of Diana Lefroy, and then he shrugged. He had been in equally bad spots before, with Bill, and they had come through them. Why not again?

Larramy was leading the way along the left-hand passage, which—Dawlish reckoned—led to rooms which overlooked the main road. At the second door the big man stopped, and Kramm went forward, taking keys from his pocket. The door was opened, and Larramy stepped through. Dawlish and Farningham, each with a gun in his ribs, followed.

Betty was sitting on a camp bed, with her legs beneath her, one elbow leaning on a pillow, and supporting her body. There was a torn magazine on her knees, and the poise looked natural and was certainly charming—she was surprisingly lovely, Dawlish thought, at the least expected times.

A studied pose, of course.

She intended to appear indifferent, and she would have succeeded but for the arrival of Dawlish and Farningham. Dawlish saw her eyes widen in dismay, heard the sharp intake of her breath. She stood up in a single, easy motion, and the magazine dropped to the floor.

"Pat—"

"Sure—Dawlish!" snapped Larramy. "And he hasn't come to waste words. Get them out, Dawlish."

Dawlish said, very slowly: "Betty, I don't know what these people want you to do, but you'll have to agreee, or—" he shrugged, and his face looked haggard. Sounding hopeless, he went on: "Well, they've got us where they want us, Betty."

Her lips tightened, slowly.

"I—see. You're to persuade me to speak to save your own life, is that it?" The words would have seemed melodramatic but for the slow, passionless utterance, and the look of utter contempt in her eyes. Dawlish warmed towards her, and yet even then the main question in his mind was: *What did she know?*

He laughed, not with humour.

"A wrong guess, Betty; Bill and I are for the long jump anyhow. This is for your sake—or good, call it what you like. You can't help by keeping quiet."

"You think not?" Her expression was cold, as if she did not believe him, and suddenly he wanted to kick her for her obstinacy. An absurd thought, and yet for a split-second he had imagined her drugged—drugged so that she would want more, so that the craving would become unbearable.

"I'm sure," said Dawlish.

"If you can't do better than that—" Larramy started, but Dawlish cut him short.

"I'll handle it, thanks. I—" he clenched his hands, so that the fingers touched the sleeves, and then raised them. "Betty, don't go in for mock-heroics, these people—"

She stopped him with a quick movement of her hand, and Larramy stared at her. At which moment Pat Dawlish winked, deliberately and with apparent amusement. He turned his head, seeing that the two gunmen were away from the door, standing close to him, and in that moment he played his trump card.

His thumb nail scraped on a vesta match taken from his right sleeve, and the match flared. From his left hand a small coil of magnesium tape showed, concealed until that moment up his left sleeve. Before they could move to stop him he put the match to the tape, and the white flare was almost instantaneous. Prepared for it, he closed his eyes and jumped backwards. He cannoned into either Schuster or Kramm, sending the man sprawling, and heard the clatter of an automatic on the lino-covered floor. His foot touched the automatic, he stooped down for it, clutched it and then someone cannoned into him. The safety-catch was off, a sharp *crack*! echoed through the room—and then he reached the door, opened his eyes widely, saw Larramy, Schuster and Kramm still reeling, dazzled and temporarily blinded by the white flare. The window had been smashed by the shot, and there was a cut on Farningham's right hand.

Betty was standing still, but swaying on her feet, her hands at her eyes.

"Damned smart!" Farningham muttered. He seemed to be less affected by the glare than any of the others, for he saw well enough to snatch Larramy's gun from his shoulder-holster and to crack his right fist into Larramy's face. As the man reeled back, Schuster grabbed for his gun, also on the floor. Dawlish wasted no time, but fired—and Schuster leapt back, blood spurting from his right wrist.

"Shut that door!" snapped Dawlish. "Watch 'em, Bill!"

He stepped swiftly to the window, and cracked it with the butt of his gun, breaking the pane of glass completely. Dawlish leaned out, and his voice travelled far:

"Morely—get in fast!"

There was a shout from the road. Men burst suddenly into a run, although he could not see them. He felt a sharp relief searing through him, greater than he fully realised, and as he turned back into the room his grin was lopsided.

"All hunky-dory," he said. "Gentlemen of Clunes, all ready on a plate."

And then from outside the room he heard the laugh, a high-pitched, cackling laughter which seemed insane. For some seconds he stood rigid; then he crossed to the door. Farningham had the three men covered, Betty was sitting on the edge of the bed, the colour drained from her face and her eyes filled with tears brought by the flash.

He flung the door open—

As he did so a tongue of flame shot into the room from the passage—the passage which had seemed empty five minutes before was now a blazing inferno.

And the laughter cackled again.

CHAPTER XXVII

MA FINNIGAN

The shock was enough to send Dawlish back and off his balance.

The flames leapt into the room, caught at a rickety bamboo table, and sent it crackling. Farningham jumped for the table and flung it outside, heedless of scorched hands. He banged the door to, and although in that moment he had given Larramy and the others a chance of making a break, it had not been taken. Larramy was standing against the wall, terror in his eyes.

"Can we make it?" Dawlish asked, his expression bleak.

"Not that way—the whole passage is blazing." Farningham was pale but spoke casually enough.

"Quick work, petrol or something like it. That laugh—"

"Someone's crazy—I'm not sure we aren't all," said Dawlish. "I'll try to get them from outside." He reached the window again, and called—but cars were moving swiftly along the road, the hum of their engines drowning the sound of his voice. Morely was moving a strong force of men into the grounds, it was almost impossible to attract attention. Dawlish felt a savage inward anger, anger at the thought that this could have gone wrong at the last moment. But the anger went, he was calculating the chances. Farningham seemed to read his mind.

"Not a hope, this is the third floor."

"I'm trying," said Dawlish briefly. "Keep them under your eye." He worked deliberately at the rest of the glass in the window, smashing every splinter away. Farningham herded Larramy, Schuster and Kramm into one corner, away from Betty, who was staring at Dawlish with her lips working.

"What—what are you going to do?"

"Try a spot of house-mountaineering," said Dawlish and he sounded cheerful. "There's help quite close, old lady—don't let it worry you too much."

"But surely the passage is all right."

As she spoke there was a crack like a revolver shot from the door, and a panel of wood split open. Flame leapt through again and as Dawlish hoisted himself to the window level, the panel was burnt right out. The crackling and roaring of the flames was all they could hear—and the air suddenly seemed too warm to breathe.

All they could see through the panel was a mass of red and yellow flames.

Dawlish climbed outside, his figure illuminated by the light from the door.

Could he get down?

He groped downwards with his right foot, found a pipe, and tested it with his weight. It seemed to offer hold, and he lowered himself to it gradually. It took time, and the precious seconds meant less chance for the others in the room. He gritted his teeth, fighting against impatience which could bring disaster. Through a false step. He reached the window immediately below—and as he did so a tongue of flame leapt through it, showing everything about him clearly for a moment.

And showing him the drain-pipe running straight to the ground, a yard to his right.

Just within reach.

His right hand touched the pipe, and gripped it. He let his body sag towards it, pressing himself close to the wall as he went. For a perilous moment he hung in mid-air, only clutching the pipe one-handed—

It sagged.

Dawlish's heart seemed to drop. He had a moment of dreadful fear: and then he brought his left hand over, and was able to put some of his weight on a lower section of the pipe. He steadied himself, and then began to go downwards slowly.

Too slowly—

Suddenly a beam of light shot upwards, he saw it moving on the wall close to him, and the next moment he was in the beam. He heard voices, none of which he recognised, and saw that he had only two yards to go. He made one of them, and the dropped. As he touched the ground two men rushed him.

"Take it steady, now!" The official bark of a policeman's voice, the sight of the man's uniform, made Dawlish feel light-headed for a moment. Two hands gripped his shoulders, a torch was shone in his face.

"Lord! It's Mr. Dawlish!"

A man from the Yard, a man who recognised him!

Dawlish drew a deep breath and gasped:

"Run—an escape—that window. Straight above—this. Send—three-four men. Make it—fast."

"Yes, sir!" The Yard man swung round, and in the flashing beams of torches, more frequent now, Dawlish saw that a fire-engine was actually in the grounds. He saw the crew running an escape-ladder up to the window—and he had an absurd desire to sing.

"'Ave a drop, sir?" A man approached him, carrying a whisky flask. Dawlish put the open neck to his lips, took a swallow of the neat spirit and felt much steadier.

"Thanks. Is Sir Archibald here?"

"Gone to the front of the house, sir."

"Thanks, I'll join him." Dawlish went towards the front entrance, surprised at the unsteadiness of his legs. But he reached the doorway, from which a light glowed faintly. Inside were two uniformed policemen, and as Dawlish went in they barred his path.

"No one's to come in, sir."

"I—" Dawlish bit back on a sharp retort, and was going for his identification card when he heard Trivett's voice.

"Dawlish! Thank God you're all right!"

"All right will serve," said Dawlish, "and I think the others will be. But the top of the house is an inferno."

"I know—" as he drew nearer, Dawlish saw that Trivett's face was blackened, that his collar was scorched. "We can't save the place, it's spreading like the devil. There are three men holding out in the cellar, and others—"

He broke off.

Screams came from above, and then a high-pitched cackling laugh, the laughter that Dawlish had heard before. There were heavy footsteps and shouts—and then a weird caricature of a woman appeared on the first landing—a caricature of tragedy too, for her clothes were alight at the back. Her face was working; her hands were raised towards the ceiling. She stumbled as she reached the first stair, recovered herself, and came running down. Her dress was jet-black, her face, distorted though it was, was deathly pale.

She was screaming:

"Members, the Members, I'll give them Members!"

She broke again into that high-pitched, insane laughter—and by then she was at the foot of the stairs, and Dawlish and Trivett were barring her path. Dawlish had his coat off, planning to wrap it about her to smother the flames.

He stopped her, but her hands clawed at his cheeks and eyes, her legs kicked at him. The fury of her rush carried him to the ground, and yet the woman kept on her feet, wrenching herself away from him. She tripped Trivett as the Inspector tried to grab her, and rushed for the door.

"Members, Members, I'll give them Members!"

The two uniformed men closed on her. One stuck out his foot and she stumbled over it and went sprawling as Dawlish picked himself up. But she seemed to be made of indiarubber, for she bounced up again and rushed into the grounds. She was alight now from head to foot, a veritable pillar of flame.

Dawlish saw half a dozen men rush towards her. She stopped as though she knew she could not get past that number, then turned and ran back to the house. Her face was dreadful: her hair, piled up at the top of her head, a burst of vivid flame. Screaming, she pitched forward on her face—and as the flames enveloped her she lashed so wildly about her that she stopped anyone getting near enough to help.

Dawlish felt sick.

Trivett said: "My God, what an end! She deserved a bad one, but that was too bad."

"You knew her?" Dawlish stared at him.

"Yes, a Ma Finnigan. Not a nice creature, but she's been missing for some years."

Dawlish frowned. "Queer thing—these people seem to use a number of one-time crooks, Triv. Anyhow, it doesn't seem to make much difference. How many others have you found?"

"Just the three in the cellar, and Grayson or Bilson in one

of the rooms. He was in bed, but he tried to get his gun—and didn't." Trivett shrugged. "They're going through the other rooms now, and the A.C.'s with them. Where are—?"

"Farningham and Betty?" Dawlish said. "Outside by now, I hope. My wild-eyed customer was upstairs, with a couple of roughnecks. With luck, they're also down and still breathing. It might be an idea if I worked on the man myself; he won't talk easily."

Trivett stared. "Look here—"

"Regulations, I know. But I could spirit him away."

Trivett hesitated, then shrugged. "He's your prisoner, Dawlish. But don't turn him into a corpse."

This business, thought Dawlish, was making even Trivett throw regulations overboard, and there was some humour in the thought. He hurried outside again, and now the darkness was relieved by the reflected glow from the fire, which had taken hold of the whole top of the house. In it he could see the waiting men clearly—and by the drain-pipe which had been so vital, the fire-escape and the little huddle of people about it.

He saw Betty.

Farningham was there, *and* the pale-faced man.

Dawlish hurried towards them, and as he went he was thinking of the woman who had run screaming, with the word 'Members' so often on her lips.

And he wondered whether his man could amplify that cryptic utterance.

CHAPTER XXVIII

DID LARRAMY LIE?

Farningham's clothes were scorched and his hair was singed, and there was a rent in Lady Betty's blouse. But both of them were on their feet, and the girl was actually smiling.

Dawlish reached them and called them aside. The man whose name he did not know was standing still, with handcuffs on his wrists. Schuster and Kramm were in the same predicament, but they seemed too scared to worry about it.

The wild eyes of Larramy did not suggest fear so much as rage.

"A word," Dawlish said *sotto voce*. "Our work's only just starting, Bill—we're going to try to squeeze news out of the big shot. Betty, tie yourself to the biggest policeman in sight and don't let him lose you."

She laughed, a trifle hysterically.

"I've been lost quite enough, thanks."

"Then show you've learned your lesson," said Dawlish. He pulled her ear, an oddly intimate warming little gesture, then murmured to the policeman from the Yard who had recognised him:

"Who's the big prisoner—do you know?"

"Not to know him, sir; a local man says he's a Mr. Larramy."

"Thanks. I want Mr. Larramy for a short while, for Inspector Trivett."

"Your prisoner, sir."

"Thanks again," Dawlish jerked his head towards Larramy, and Farningham stepped with him to the big man's side. Dawlish gripped his forearm. "Larramy, you and I are going to talk."

Larramy swore. "You. . . !"

"Now that's not nice. I saved your life," said Dawlish, but his voice was sharp. He forced the man to move, not towards the house but in the direction of the thick yew-hedge. Between it and the house where a number of tall trees, completely in the shadows. The noise from the house itself, the leaping flames from the roof, and the sight of men silhouetted against the glare, seemed a long way off to Patrick Dawlish.

He stopped near the hedge.

"This'll do, Bill. Now, Larramy, you're going to talk, and if you're slow about it you're going to get hurt. They're too busy over by the house to worry about a scream or two."

"You go to hell!"

"I don't like doing this," said Dawlish.

It was true, although the blow he delivered to Larramy's chin was sharp and painful and was intended to be. Larramy staggered, might have fallen, but for Farningham's restraining hand.

"There's too much at stake for foolery." Dawlish's voice was hard. "I'm going to get your story, Larramy, if I have to flay the skin off your back. First—who are the Members?"

He might have dropped a bomb.

Larramy started back. His lips opened; his eyes showed sheer stupefaction. He raised his handcuffed wrists, as though to ward off a blow, and gasped:

"You know—about *them*?"

"It seems like it." Dawlish was filled with a warm glow of exhilaration. The woman had known what she was screaming about: the word meant something vital. "Who are they?"

"Oh—God! Dawlish, I don't know, I swear I don't know! If I did I'd talk—I might get off lighter! I *don't know them!* They come here in a closed car, they're always disguised; I've worked for them for years and never seen their real faces!" The words were pouring from the man now, and his forehead was beaded with sweat, his lips working. "Dawlish, I'm telling you God's truth—I don't know who they are!"

"How often do they come?"

"Sometimes—sometimes once a week, sometimes they'll go a couple of months without meeting. They—they ran the drug racket; Misslethwaites was their place. I told them they should not have pulled that mug's trick—I didn't know a thing about it!"

"Go on," said Dawlish.

"I can't, I tell you! They were mad about getting those brushes back; I had three-four men who used guns, and they told me to get them busy. The Grey's worked for them, not for me. I'm not responsible for anything the Greys did!"

"You were going out to-night," said Dawlish. "Right now, do you remember?"

Larry's face worked. "I—I was travelling to Southampton. I'm directing a hold-up of a goods train; it's being wrecked to-night, I—"

Dawlish snapped: "Which one?"

"It—it's due to leave the docks at one o'clock. There are a dozen men near the central station, on a waste patch of land there." Now that he had cracked, Larramy had lost every ounce of self-control, his abjectness and anxiety to talk were contemptible—and yet they seemed to prove that he was genuine. Dawlish's head was reeling under the implications of the statement, and he snapped:

"Any others?"

"I—I think so; Liverpool, Harwich—I don't know much about them. Southampton was my job."

"Where do the men stay?"

"God!" moaned Larramy. "Listen, Dawlish, I'm telling you I don't know, and that's fact. I swear to God it's the truth! I didn't know they'd *got* others until to-day—three hundred, they told me. I've been on the small stuff, helping to get the drugs around. But I know one thing—"

"Get it out."

Larramy drew a deep breath, and then his voice was quieter, he seemed to regain something of his self-control:

"Listen, Dawlish, will you put me in as good as you can with the police if I talk?"

"We'll see—talk first."

"I'm damned if I will!"

Dawlish struck him again, and this time he was not sorry about it. Listening to the plan to hold up goods trains, he had realised the utter callousness of the man standing there, and had thought again of the outrage in Piccadilly. Larramy was getting off far more lightly than he deserved.

He had swayed at the blow. Farningham stopped him from falling and punched him lightly in the small of the back. Larramy gasped:

"Stop—stop it, Dawlish! I—they're working something at Whitehall—something big: they've been talking about it for months. They've got a lot of the permanent officials under drugs; they can do practically what they like. Clavering's always held a tight hand on a lot of it—I don't know what. But they've got rid of him, or they think they have."

"Think is right!" snapped Dawlish. "All right, God help you if you've lied. Bill, hand him over to the police and wait for me at the gates." He hurried towards the house again, pushing his way through police and firemen.

While he had been talking to Larramy, the fire had grown fiercer. The light was a lurid glare, now, and debris was beginning to fall from the roof.

Morely was with Trivett on the steps.

"We're getting everything we can out," said Morely, as Dawlish came up. "The study's emptied. You've done a good job here, Dawlish, thank God."

"I hope to do better," said Dawlish. The police were emptying the place of furniture, and he realised that there was no time for searching the house before it was razed by the flames. "A word where we can't be heard, Morely. And you, Triv." He smiled, but bleakly.

"Well?" Morely looked intense; his eyes were haggard.

"Larramy—my wild-eyed gent—has talked. He was to have gone down to Southampton to help raid a goods train to-night, there are a dozen other men there for the job. Other parties are on similar jobs at Liverpool, Harwich, and possibly other places."

Morely stared: "My God, Dawlish, if it's true it's disastrous."

"It's true all right. More, he says that his employers are planning something at Whitehall, and that Clavering was in the way. A goodly proportion of officials are nicely doped. The only thing," went on Dawlish thoughtfully, "which might not have been the truth was his assurance that he doesn't know who his employers are. Like Ma Finnigan, he calls them the Members. Four of them, he says."

"I'll get to a 'phone," Morely said. "Better come with me— we'll get straight back to Westminster. Keep things under your eye here, Trivett. Have all the papers scrutinised as quickly as you can and report if there's anything unusual." Morely turned, and Dawlish fell in by his side. "Dawlish, do you realise what you've told me?"

"I do. They want the Home Secretary out of the way because Clavering's a man who will handle things personally—that's why they wanted to get him out of the Cabinet years ago, why he's not popular. Our gents aren't after the new man: they're just intent on getting Clavering out of the way. And obviously they haven't much time to work in; whatever it is will come quickly now. Destroying or derailing goods trains explains something, although I'm damned if I know what. What are you going to do?"

"'Phone direct to 10 Downing Street. I'm not wasting time going through Knighton."

"Knighton won't be pleased, but you're wise. Were those two clubs raided?"

"Clubs? Oh, yes. Nothing to show at all."

"Did Adams turn up?"

"No, not yet."

"He won't," said Dawlish, with an odd conviction. He stopped quite still, and he seemed to see the face of Doc Sloane as the man had died. Morely glanced at him, prepared to be irritable, but checked the comment that sprang to his lips.

"What's the matter?"

"Just an idea, old man, which might be useful a bit later on. Grayson and Ankrett?"

"They claim to be flabbergasted," said Morely, "and I don't think they're in on the business. They've been questioned by the Home Office people, and they're being shadowed. I suppose," he added dryly, "you're going to tell me that they'll disappear into thin air."

"I wouldn't be surprised," said Dawlish. "The Members, Morely—what does it mean to you?"

"A tomfool nickname," said Morely. "Call 'em Number One, Two and Three if you care to—" he broke off, for they were just outside the front door of a house near Clunes—a house which had been emptied because of the raid. "We've made this temporary headquarters. I can 'phone from here."

"Right. I'll be at the gate." Dawlish walked back quickly along the drive, and at the head of it he saw Farningham. By that time, the fire at Clunes was at its height. There was a lurid glare all round, and the reddish glow showed Farningham's tousled hair and rugged features. Dawlish grinned.

"Neither of us looks respectable, old man, and we're not in favour. Or at least we're not going to be. In plain language I'm going to do a flit."

"Oh, Lord!" groaned Farningham. "Why and where to?"

"London town. What does 'Members' mean to you?"

"Melodrama," said Farningham, "but isn't it all?"

Dawlish chuckled. "That's two of you. Of course, I may be wrong, but club members might fit the bill. They're members of something—all soubriquets have a derivative, and this one has. Members of what?"

"Your head's turned, old man. A good night's sleep, and then—"

"*After* this show's over," said Dawlish.

Farningham started. "After? Are you suggesting it'll be over to-night?"

"Early to-morrow, barring accidents."

"Then you know—"

"The sad thing is," said Dawlish, "I'm still indulging in fancies and that's why we're doing a little more work on our own. Be patient for an hour or two more—and you drive, by the way. The card will get us a car."

Morely's signature succeeded. A police car was put at their disposal, and with Farningham at the wheel they drove towards London. And on their heels was another car, which picked them up just outside the police cordon.

In it was a man with a black beard; a beard that was patently false.

CHAPTER XXIX

TO WHAT END?

Sheer instinct told Dawlish that the affair was fast reaching its climax: and this time he did not feel afraid that things would go wrong. But the possibility remained: he had to act fast and turn his fancies into facts—and there were vital things which he was convinced would be better done in person, with Farningham. Once they were finished Morely could know; the final act would start. He did not believe that the Members would succeed in what they were trying to do, but only vaguely did he comprehend the end they had in mind.

He had to ascertain that first.

Afterwards it rested with others, but he doubted whether those others could do what he was attempting—for the simple but sufficient reason that they would not adopt his methods. There was a double danger—from the Members, and from a too-cautious police attitude; he believed he could handle both.

He was sitting next to Farningham, a dishevelled, grimy figure, with a smut the size of a shilling on the side of his nose, and one of his eyebrows completely blacked-over. His lips were curved, and he seemed to be smiling dreamily.

Farningham started suddenly, and exploded: "Pat, you damned fool! You haven't found what Lady Betty knew; the whole thing might turn on it."

"The omission was deliberate," said Dawlish.

Farningham breathed heavily. "You're an irritating beggar. What was the idea?"

"I didn't want to know, yet," said Dawlish. "It might be necessary to tell Morely, and it could conceivably get her into disrepute, and we wouldn't like that."

"Are you talking out of the back of your neck *all* the time? If there's one thing certain, she's not in it."

"I hope not," said Dawlish. "Certainly I hope not, old man. However, she certainly knows something or friend Larramy would not be so anxious to make her talk. However—you miss a fairly obvious fact, Bill. Larramy was a big shot but certainly not *the* Big Shot. He wanted the information from her, and I fancy for himself. Therefore the probability is that it concerns the Members."

"Meaning—" Farningham's tone showed his scepticism— "that Betty knows more about the Members than Larramy?"

"No. Meaning she knows something about them that Larramy doesn't, an entirely different matter. Patience, Bill, I haven't worked it all out yet. We're going to have another look-see at Chloë's flat: I think it will help. Oh, I think it will help a lot!" Dawlish chuckled, and Farningham drove for some minutes in silence. It was as he turned into the maze of streets between Sloane Square and Victoria that he said resignedly:

"I suppose you know what you're doing—and I suppose you know a car's been on our tail for the last twenty minutes."

"Twenty-five minutes," said Dawlish promptly. "It's precisely why I came alone, and without any whisper to Morely. We want that Big Shot, Bill, and we'd have scared him away had we been trailed by the police. You collected another gun, I take it?

"Yes."

"Fine. And I provided myself with a key, we don't want a lot of bother getting into Chloë's flat again. Don't miss the turning in the dark, old son."

"I won't," said Farningham. He looked into the mirror and saw the lights of the following car, then turned left. He overshot de Mond Mansions, and backed into the short drive-way: the other car also drove past, slowly.

"Look the other way," said Dawlish, "don't tell him that we're quite so curious." He opened the door and climbed out, and as Farningham joined him in the darkened entrance porch, he gripped his friend's arm. "Last act, Bill. Still with me?"

"Don't be a fool."

"Right." Dawlish stepped into the hall. There was complete silence in the building. He was smiling a little to himself as he pushed the key into the door, hesitated, and then pushed it open sharply. Complete darkness met them, and they stepped through.

And then the light flashed on.

Farningham gasped: Dawlish stood quite still.

Three men, two bearded and one clean-shaven, were sitting in front of them, and all were in evening-dress. At their sides were two gunmen, their automatics fitted with silencers and pointing towards Dawlish and Farningham. On a settee by the curtained window was Sir Louis Morrell, but a Morrell very different from the *beau* so well known to the illustrated weeklies and Mayfair *salons*. His face was beaded with sweat, his crinkly hair awry; his shirt—he wore no coat and waist-coat—gaped open at the chest, and on that were two small, red marks.

Cigarette burns, Dawlish knew.

The man whose beard and hair were grey, and whom

Larramy knew as Two, was in the middle of the trio, and he spoke gently—the voice Dawlish had heard when Clavering had been faced with the ultimatum.

"Well, Dawlish—you make the same mistake too often, don't you?"

Dawlish said stiffly: "You think so?"

"I'm quite sure," said Two gently. "This time you will not get away, it was so foolish of you to come on your own. You were watched from the time you came out of the attic, and our agent assures us that you said no word of this little visit—anxious, I suppose, to make sure that your friends do not meet trouble."

"It might be." Dawlish still spoke stiffly, as if he were suffering from a shock which was the last he had expected.

"A little perturbed, I see," said the grey-bearded man. "It's understandable, but you have a reputation for keeping your poise so well. I'm almost disappointed. I—"

Dawlish smiled for the first time.

"Don't be that, whatever else. You've enough disappointments to come. You needn't torture Morrell, you know—he hasn't got the brushes. And if he had he'd talk more easily if you kept him short of snow for a few days—one of your own victims, and you didn't know he was an addict! Too bad," drawled Patrick Dawlish. And now his attitude was confident; he seemed to lounge, inwardly to laugh.

Number One snapped: "How do you know Morrell hasn't got them?"

"A little bird whispered to me—and also told me who had."

The words set all three Members bolt upright in their chairs

"Where are they?" snapped One.

"All in good time," said Dawlish. "Morrell had them, Jeffery stole them—and incidentally stole them just because they were silver-backed brushes; Morrell didn't pay him too well. And then our cut-throat visited Jeffery and collared the brushes. Incidentally the same cut-throat—no two men could do a vile job like that—later visited my flat and killed two admirable fellows, which was not a nice thing to do. He did it so cleverly both times—he hoped to make the police start thinking seriously about me, but he didn't realise that although they dislike my methods they approve of my morals. However, Cut-throat is one of your associates, my Members—a man who stole the brushes and what is in them but did not take you into his confidence. I wouldn't like to suggest that he preferred to have the stuff to use to coerce you at a later date, but it might have happened. Or mightn't it?"

Dawlish beamed, as if this was the best joke in the world, and certainly his words had caused consternation. The Members were on their feet, and Number Two stepped forward, his hand raised and clenched.

"I shouldn't," Dawlish said.

Perhaps the expression in his eyes stopped the blow, although Farningham had expected it to come, and was sick at heart. Dawlish knew—or guessed—something he had not confided, but playing a cat-and-mouse game with these people was simply inviting murder. There was a sinking feeling deep down in Bill Farningham. Dawlish was gambling—Dawlish could not always win. But he demanded admiration, even unwilling admiration.

Like a man in a dream, Farningham saw Morrell, his forehead glistening, leaning forward and staring tensely, saw the automatics in the hands of the gunmen—and the rage in the eyes of the three men whom the burning woman at Wimbledon had called the Members.

"Who is the man?" snapped Number Two. "Who has the brushes?"

"I don't know his name," said Dawlish amiably. "Not his real name." He was watching the other lynx-eyed, knew what he was dicing with death, yet saw no other way of getting at the whole truth. "He's probably thrown the brushes away; the letters inside are what matters. Foolish of you to put your signatures to such damning documents—"

Farningham believed the man would crash his fist into Dawlish's face. He might have done, but Three interrupted, restraining Two and speaking sharply.

"How do you know about the letters, Dawlish?"

"Documents sounds so much more imposing," Dawlish's voice was easy but his body was rigid, as if prepared for immediate action. Farningham had an impression that he was listening for something. "Four Members—Members at one time of the Worshipful Company of Silversmiths, of course. Which of you is Ankrett? And which is Grayson?"

Number One snapped: "You swine! Grayson, have him put away at once; he knows, he—"

He spoke to Number Two, and Dawlish laughed, a short, sharp sound.

"So you're Ankrett, that amiable peer. And you—" he mocked the grey-bearded man in front of him—"are Mortimer Grayson. I can't name your third member, and Charles Mullinger Adams isn't here, is he? Not yet. The fourth Member, the travelling Member who controlled the shipments of drugs and some of the selling of it. The organising mind, I fancy, our Charles Mullinger Adams—and Misslethwaites provided such excellent cover while it lasted. Was it the managing-director of Misslethwaites who planned the large-scale crimes, I wonder? Who was prepared to make chaos up and down the country? Who organised several hundred men for that purpose, but so carefully that Larramy did not realise what was happening under his nose? Was it the Fourth Member who worked the dope into Whitehall, ostentatiously in the Foreign Office and the Admiralty to get the police concentrating on the wrong angle, while the real efforts were directed towards the Home Office? The Fourth Member who realised that Clavering, keeping everything under his personal supervision so much, had to be removed somehow—and discovered the skeleton in Clavering's cupboard?"

Ankrett—the peer *was* Number One—raised his voice again. He sounded panic-stricken.

"Grayson, for God's sake finish him!"

"Let him talk," said Mortimer Grayson slowly. "We'll know just what he thinks he knows before he's finished. Go on, Dawlish."

Dawlish smiled. "Thanks. There's no 'thinking' about it. It's all by deduction and constructive application. *Why* cause an upheaval in the Arcade instead of clearing out as soon as I was known to have been there, and would be likely to send the police? *Why* arrange for troubles with trains? *Why* hold a large number of men ready for other disturbances? *Why* try to get virtual control of the Home Office? *Why* sell drugs so fast in London that ten or fifteen per cent of the wealthy population take it, and thus need it?"

He paused, and the silence seemed to hum. Farningham was staring, Morrell seemed to have forgotten whatever he had suffered and was leaning forward, his heavy eyes wide-open. It was Number Three who broke the silence.

"Well, Dawlish—why?"

"Because the Home Office controls commodity prices," said Patrick Dawlish, and his voice was low-pitched and yet filled every corner of the room. "Foodstuffs, clothing, metals—all commodities. Any member of the Stock Exchange would know that—any man or men with capital enough could buy considerable shares of commodity companies; and, with prices soaring far above raw material costs, could make a fantastic fortune. It was so clever, wasn't it? Drugs in high places to keep Government restrictions from getting worrying—drugs in so many other places to make it look as though it was a drug-wave. Hold-ups and large scale crime to present an ostensible reason for the rise in prices—one the House and the public would swallow. The Arcade affair to show the authorities how threatening the crime-wave was: how poor commodity stock-holders were fighting to keep prices as low as possible, while every official who could inspect figures was drugged enough to make sure he would raise no complaints, make no exhaustive inquiries. So water-tight, wasn't it?"

Farningham's head reeled.

Dawlish had spoken slowly, every word taking effect, had drawn a picture of a price-ramp that was almost beyond comprehension, of a profiteering organisation setting out deliberately, with diabolical cunning, to put prices at a level which made fantastic fortunes possible.

Dawlish said easily:

"Profiteering de-luxe. And it might have worked."

Ankrett's lips were working.

"Grayson, for God's sake—"

"You said that before," said Dawlish.

Grayson, or Number Two, said gently:

"Very clever, Dawlish, and quite accurate—I don't see how you reached the conclusions, but that's of no account. You've guessed a lot, for instance—you didn't know the papers in the brushes contained our individual suggestions while we were working this thing up—quite convincing evidence of our individual parts. However, you make one miscalculation— it *will* work. You've made your guess, and you came here to confirm it, a thing you could only do yourself. Right?"

"Nicely judged," admitted Patrick Dawlish.

"But it made it difficult for you to make sure of getting away," said Grayson suavely. "In fact impossible. You may stop one or two of our early efforts, Larramy was to have been busy tonight, for instance, but for the rest—" he shrugged. "I'm almost sorry to see you go, Dawlish."

"Too conventional," said Dawlish. "You ought to be nice and melodramatic, like Ankrett, it might frighten me. On the other hand, it might not. Your Fourth Member, gentlemen—forgotten him? He's got evidence, you know: *he* murdered Jeffery for the brushes, *he's* been concentrating on getting me put away. He'll have you nicely in a corner, he can take whatever share he likes instead of a humble fourth. He—"

And then the door swung open.

Dawlish had been alert for the slightest sound, and heard the first turn of the handle. He did not see the black-bearded man enter with a gun in his hand, but he did see every eye turned towards the door. It was then he acted, taking his life in his hands. He did not move, except to snatch his gun from his pocket, and he kept his finger on the trigger, firing low. Ankrett and Grayson went down, with the two gunmen, and then Dawlish leapt to one side. Farningham snatched at his gun but did not use it, for Dawlish sent him flying with a sweep of his mighty arm. For a few seconds there was bedlam; men gasping and moaning, blood spilling—only Number Three and the new-corner, Number Four, on their feet, facing each other.

Four snapped: "He was lying, he—"

He turned his gun towards Dawlish, and the flame and lead streamed out, biting into Dawlish's back as he moved. Dawlish pitched forward on to the settee. Farningham saw him and felt a dreadful fear.

Dawlish muttered into Morrell's ear:

"Another gun—in my pocket. Get the man by the door."

And Morrell acted, covered by Dawlish's body. The man in the doorway was moving forward when the bullets bit into his side, and he coughed and staggered. Three swung round—and Farningham fired from the floor, catching the man's thigh and pitching him forward. Farningham leapt towards Dawlish.

And Dawlish, his face twisted in pain, gasped:

"All right, old man. Bruises only—good things, chain waistcoats! Watch the—swine—and watch the—door. His wife—may come—"

Farningham stared: "Whose wife?"

"Colonel—Adams. Nice—fellow! Man who poisoned—Doc Sloane's whisky. God, my—back!" Dawlish stretched along the settee, his lips set and twisted.

And then Farningham saw that the black beard of the man who had entered—who had followed them from Wimbledon although Farningham did not know it then—had been dislodged, with the moustache; and he saw the once-genial face of Chloë Farrimond's nextdoor neighbour.

Colonel Adams!

As he stared, Farningham felt the fantasy of the last few minutes. That whirlwind sharpshooting which Dawlish had relied on, knowing that when he accused Number Four the man would come in if he had been listening! Dawlish had judged the psychology of them all to a nicety, but the gamble made Farningham sweat.

But not so much as the whirring sound from one of the walls.

He swung round—to see the wall opening and the woman standing there. Mrs. Adams, with a gun in her hand—and two men just behind her, also armed.

CHAPTER XXX

OF MEN AND THEIR LADIES

For a split-second Farningham felt the hopelessness of trying to avoid death. The guns were raised and his was lowered. He jerked his arm up—but even as he jerked, a little glass phial flew from Dawlish's hand and smashed in the woman's face. The cloud of ammonia gas from it sent her reeling back, the gunmen with her, as Dawlish shouted:

"Let 'em have it, Bill!"

Farningham fired, low to avoid killing. Through the cloud of gas which started to sting his own eyes and mouth, he saw the woman fall, and the men immediately afterwards. He staggered a little and tears welled in his eyes, as Dawlish moved slowly from his couch, his back easier.

"I'll 'phone the Yard," he said. "From Adams's flat. I wondered what the trick was here; the sliding door was clever. I wonder if Chloë knew it was put in when she was having her room made sound-proof?"

Farningham grunted, his mouth too painful for speech. But Morrell was farther away from the gas and unaffected. He gripped Dawlish's arm, and his eyes looked haggard.

"She knew, Dawlish—but she couldn't help what she did, I'll swear to that!"

Dawlish grinned crookedly. "Quite sure?"

"Yes, I—" Morrell drew a deep breath, and made a praiseworthy effort to regain his poise. "Dawlish, Miss Farrimond was—was an habitual taker of cocaine; anything she did was under the influence of it, I know. Adams started her on it, forced her to distribute cocaine among—among her friends."

"I—see," said Dawlish, and the news was what he had angled for. It explained Larramy's "she'll be in prison for years," but it did not explain Morrell's part. He shrugged—and wished he had not, for the bruises in the small of his back were agonising when he moved. "It might go over, Morrell, but your part will want some explaining."

The knight stared. "*My* part? Dawlish, I have tried in every way possible to get her out of the man's control! I—" he hesitated, and Dawlish saw a strange alteration in his expression; a quiet dignity, almost a serenity. "I am in love with Miss Farrimond. I hope you will not insist on my talking too fully, but I feel you deserve to know this. I would have been married but for her association with Adams, and—" Morrell hesitated, to go on very slowly: "and with Sir Arnold Clavering. She lived with him, secretly, for some years. She will do nothing now that will endanger his position. I—I admire her for it, I would not have it otherwise. And Adams, you see, has used that also to persuade her to continue operating with him. Dawlish, the torment of not knowing whether she could keep an appointment, or whether Adams kept her away, was unbearable."

Morrell turned his head, and Dawlish eased himself up slowly, looking the other way. Farningham, who had heard everything, met his eyes. Dawlish smiled, a quiet, understanding smile.

"I think I can understand, Morrell, and I'm glad to know the

Clavering angle—that puzzled me. The brushes—you bought them for sentimental reasons?"

"Of course, I had no idea what was in them. Not until Chloë tried to get them back from Cunningham without telling me—she was trying to avoid hurting me, she always does. Not until then did she know Adams had used them for these incriminating papers—which he wanted, of course, to use against his partners when the opportunity arose. The—the three men here to-night did not know he had stolen them from Jeffery; they believed I had them. It was not—pleasant."

"It could have been much worse," said Dawlish. "No one but Adams knows of Chloë's part in this business?"

"And these other people. His wife, of course. It started with his wife's friendliness with Chloë. The wife is an addict. I don't altogether blame her, but—" Morrell straightened his shoulders, "it will have to come out, of course."

Dawlish said: "Will you face it?"

"I shall wait for her," said Morrell with a quiet dignity that was impressive. "It will be best to get it over; the strain has been unbearable."

"Ye-es," said Dawlish, and then lightly: "Did you know Lady Betty Lorne?"

Morrell shrugged. "I wondered if you would guess that. I knew her slightly. She came to see me—when was it? Yesterday—it is incredible that it has happened so quickly! Her fiancé was worried about Chloë who had 'phoned him several times, and—well, I told her the position. She had no cause to worry. She wanted the brushes; of course. I told her what they contained—"

Morrell broke off, for Dawlish snapped his fingers, and his eyes were shining.

"She *knew* they were there, Larramy only suspected it—just

as well she didn't tell, but I could have told Morely without worrying."

"What on earth—" began Morrell.

"Bill knows," said Dawlish, and he laughed as he looked about the room, at the eight people on the floor, wounded, unable to move.

"Do you happen to know where they keep their gunmen," he said almost casually.

"No," said Morrell. "But I believe they keep them at various places; some I know are at a small hotel in St. John's Wood, run by a man named Askew—"

"Askew!" snapped Dawlish. "The man named on the envelope." He shrugged, and winced, and went on: "It's happened so quickly I've forgotten even that address. Morely will trace them—there are bound to be records here or at Wimbledon."

"Adams keeps them himself, in his study."

"Nice work," said Dawlish, and smiled again. But there was no humour in his eyes; his expression was suddenly bleak. "And the gas?"

"I don't know," said Morrell.

"I'll find out," said Dawlish. "Bill, keep them all in sight; they may yet try tricks."

He stepped through the sliding-door, to find himself in the lounge of the Adams's flat. As he went he realised how Adams, although seeming friendly, had kept him out of the flat when Chloë had been found, on the pretence of the cold his wife had forgotten the next day. At the back of his mind he had suspected Adams, but the suspicions had not come to a head until after Doc Sloane's murder. He saw everything slip easily into place: the key—as he had suspected—was a simple one, and unlocked all the doors. . . .

Now—

Morrell and Chloë implicated seriously, Chloë so deeply that no Court could let her go free. The Clavering-Chloë story in the Press—the trial could not be kept secret without a general outcry, that was certain.

So many things would come out that were better left unknown. Even Betty would be implicated: she would take it smiling, of course. She would do much for Andy Cunningham.

He smiled sombrely at his suspicions of Andy as he entered the study of Colonel Robert Adams. He felt weary, and his eyes were burning: he knew what he was going to do, and yet he hesitated. If Morely dreamed of it, there would be ructions.

He saw another room leading from the study, and that door was locked, but there was a key on the desk. He opened the door and stepped through—and saw a small laboratory, two gas-masks hanging on pegs, a dozen small cylinders of gas; all of them marked.

He remembered the gassing of the crowd in Piccadilly, and the list of casualties.

His lips tightened, and he picked up a small container, labelled Lewisite. He wondered in what circumstances Adams would have used the gas which killed instantaneously, and his lips were compressed in a long, thin line. He picked up a gas-mask, studied the simple mechanism of the Lewisite cylinder-cap and, carrying it with both arms, for it was heavy, went back to the room where Adams, Ankrett, Grayson and Number Three, with the woman and the gunmen, were waiting. Only Adams and Grayson were conscious, bar two of the gunmen.

Mildly curious about the identity of Number Three, Dawlish said:

"Who's the unknown, Adams?"

Adams glared. "You can go to hell."

"It will have to come out at the trial, and before," said Dawlish, and Adams swore—a stream of obscenity which seemed to colour the air. Across it came Grayson's voice:

"He was the manager at Misslethwaite's. Dawlish—" there was agony in Grayson's voice, his body was quivering as he lay stretched out on the floor. "There's a fortune in this! Just let me go—don't worry about the others: get me out of here and it's worth a hundred thousand. A hundred thousand!"

Dawlish contemplated him, his eyes narrowed.

"Just you alone, eh?"

"Yes, *yes*! I'll get the cash for you, I've got it stored."

"How were the trains to be held up?" asked Dawlish.

"Explosives on the line—but I didn't arrange that. It was Adams's work!"

"Where are the other trains due to start from? Southampton, Liverpool, Harwich and where?"

"Plymouth, Bristol and Glasgow. I'll give you full particulars, Dawlish. I know when they've timed—you're several hours to work in!"

"Drivers and stokers on those trains would have died," said Dawlish. He was still carrying the cylinder of Lewisite, and he moved towards the door. "Bill, clear out! You too, Morrell."

"What—" Farningham began.

"Get out!" snapped Dawlish roughly.

Farningham stared, and then obeyed, and Morrell followed him. Dawlish stepped closer to the door and rested the cylinder by it. He crossed to the sliding-panel, found the operating switch, and closed it. Adams was staring like a man possessed of the devil, and Grayson tried to get up, screaming at the top of his voice.

"Shut up," Dawlish said slowly. He crossed to Grayson and before the man realised what was happening, cracked him

on the back of the head. The butt of the gun brought unconsciousness immediately.

Adams began to sweat.

"I'm told it doesn't hurt," said Dawlish. "I feel almost sorry
about that, Adams."

"Why, you—"

Adams moved his right hand towards his pocket and Dawlish
jumped to one side, suspecting the presence of the second gun.
He fired from his pocket, his back giving him agony, and sent
Adam's gun flying from a shattered wrist. Adams went quiet,
staring at the cylinder.

Dawlish donned a gas-mask, walked to the door, kicked the
cylinder control-cap open, and then stepped swiftly through
into the hall.

Sir Archibald Morely, Sir Arnold Clavering, the Prime Minister
and several other Cabinet Ministers were in the room at 10,
Downing Street. So was Patrick Dawlish, and Chief Inspector
Trivett.

Dawlish had been speaking for five minutes, crisply and
clearly, and he did not intend to stop for long.

"And so gentlemen, I summarised my impressions, and as you
have heard, they were confirmed—there is ample testimony to
that effect. I have already made a full statement, which has been
signed and I believe handed to you. I understand, too, that all the
details of the organisation, and the localities in which the opera-
tives were in hiding, have been located from the code papers
which I took from the man Grey. The trains were not derailed,
and for that I can claim some credit—credit, gentlemen, which
I submit in extenuation of the fact that I gave the Members the
choice of killing themselves, or standing trial. Frankly, I hoped
they would use the Lewisite. We know that they did."

Dawlish stopped, and his sombre face was relieved by a quick, transforming smile.

"And now, gentlemen, I am in your hands, completely."

It was the Prime Minister who said quietly:

"This matter, and your report, is strictly confidential, Mr. Dawlish. I can offer my thanks, and later the Government's official thanks, for your services."

"Thank you," said Dawlish, and he was glad to shake hands.

The pressure of Sir Arnold Clavering's, a moment later, was even firmer, and Dawlish's eyes smiled into the Home Secretary's.

"So your resignation doesn't take effect, sir? Another absurd rumour in the morning's Press!"

He chuckled, and there was an echo from the others. Raising one eyebrow towards Morely, he went out, walked slowly and painfully along the street to Whitehall. As he turned into the wider thoroughfare a car drew up and Farningham jumped out—on his heels his Diana, her bronze hair sleek and lovely, her green-eyes shining.

"So you got away with it!" said Farningham, as if he could not believe his eyes.

"I was even congratulated," smiled Dawlish. "'Lo, Di. Where's Andy?"

"Waiting for you at the flat, with Morrell. Chloë's all right, and Betty'll be at the flat when we arrive, so jump in."

Dawlish jumped in, but remained thoughtful. There were several points he had learned to explain earlier mysteries. How Chloë had bought the brushes with drugs inside. Extracted the packet and believed the brushes empty when she had given them to Andy. Later she had learned that Adams, looking for a safe place to hide the papers and distrusting the other members, had used the brushes, not expecting them to be sent away: the start of the game for Dawlish.

Other things; some guessed. How Adams had followed up Morrell because of the friendship with Chloë, learned Jeffery had stolen the brushes, climbed into his room and stolen them after killing the secretary to implicate Dawlish whom he knew would soon be on the way. There was no other possible explanation; Adams would have found it easy enough to contact Jeffery, who had been robbing Morrell for some time past.

Twenty minutes later, at the flat, he looked round at Morrell, who seemed a new man; at Andy, who looked the worse for wear and Betty, who had never seemed fresher; at Farningham who was holding Diana's hand. He shrugged—and winced.

"*Blast* my back! Well—this seems a place for men and their ladies more than anything else. I'll go out for a drink. Unless there are any complaints—?"

"Complaints!" exclaimed Morrell. "My dear Dawlish!"

Betty laughed.

"I almost wish I were going to marry you instead of Andy, Pat. You're superb!"

"I'm going to see the Assistant Commissioner," grinned Dawlish, "and he won't think so."

It was half an hour before he got away, and then he walked with Morrell as far as the end of Brook Street. Morrell was going to see Chloë, and his eyes were bright in anticipation. Dawlish laughed.

"I did you more than one injustice, Morrell."

Morrell pursed his lips: "I wonder. I've invited a great deal of criticism, but—well, shall we say that this has been good for my soul?"

Dawlish frowned. "I wonder if it has for mine?"

"You did the right thing—the only thing," said Morrell soberly. "But I think you're the only man who would have contemplated doing it. You're a strange fellow, Dawlish."

And Dawlish laughed, and went to Scotland Yard to deliver up his *open sesame* card, which Morely turned over thoughtfully. The A.C. looked up and smiled gravely.

"Do you think I believe the story, Dawlish?"

"Please yourself," said Dawlish. "Facts, not fancies, my Morely; deal in them. You're not going to complain, are you?"

"I am not," said the A.C. slowly. "You were right, of course. That's the irritating part about you: you usually are! Anyhow, I can't say thanks enough—nor can Trivett. Munk's got the idea too, I think, and—" Morely's lips curved—"Jonathan Grey sent a special message from his cell—he wants to thank you."

"Vengeful to the last, was he? Who were the Greys?"

"Chemists, both of them, who started work on the drugs angle, and also developed the gas that caused the trouble in Piccadilly—a chloroform gas and simple enough to make, while taking immediate effect. Adams used them for all angles; they had a murky past, as all his men did. We've rounded up two hundred or more; all men with records. Bilson—or Grayson—is wanted for murder; Larramy's real record is the foulest thing I've heard. Ma Finnigan was wanted on a murder charge—she hadn't been out of that house for years, obviously the climax sent her mad. Poor beggar." Morely shook his head, his expression sober. Then looked up. "Well, Dawlish—?"

"Did you get the three men out of the cellar?"

"Only one came out alive, and he didn't like it. Oh, they collected the right type. Even at Whitehall—there was a man named Cautald, a permanent official, watching their interests—he's stopped watching now. Lord, it was a thorough business! The provincial branches of Misslethwaites were all crammed with drugs, which had been brought into the country over a long period. Adams ran the firm, of course, persuading Grayson and Ankrett into it. As bad a specimen as we're likely to meet."

"I'm not sorry they don't grow on trees," said Dawlish dryly.

"Hmm. Did you know that 'Colonel' Adams was identical with Charles Mullinger Adams?"

"I thought it likely when there was no male relative," said Dawlish. "Odd thing, sticking to the name. His wife backed him one hundred per cent, didn't she?"

"Judging from the records, she urged him on all the time. A clever woman. Dawlish—do you know, we hardly contacted with *any* of them during the whole investigation?"

Dawlish chuckled. "What, on neither day?"

"We *had* started before you came in," retorted Morely. "Don't say it, I know! How much did you guess, and how did you guess it?"

"Logical deduction," protested Dawlish. "Actually, most things clicked into shape when I knew Clavering was being victimised. Had you any idea of his association with Chloë?"

"I was flabbergasted," admitted Morely.

"The things our politicians can do," said Dawlish. "It's a censorious world, old man, that's the cause of half the trouble. Between you and me, I'm surprised how right I was."

Morely shrugged. "Luck, intelligence or intuition—whichever it is, you've got plenty. By the way—" he pushed a cardboard box across his desk—"a present from Scotland Yard. We shan't need them for Exhibit 'A' as there's no trial."

"The brushes?" Dawlish raised an eyebrow. "Thanks, old man, I'll frame them. Odd thing is, I wasn't sure whether they contained anything. I assumed they did and asked myself what could be making all the rumpus. Queer, isn't it?"

"I'll call it uncanny," said Sir Archibald Morely. And when Dawlish had gone, he repeated the word to himself—and was not the only friend of Patrick Dawlish's who thought the same thing.

To all of which, Dawlish was oblivious. There were no more problems, he told himself cheerfully. And was glad, since any mental effort would be a strain. And then he saw two men in uniform standing by his car. "Traffic wardens," he said to himself, and smiled as he reached, unthinkingly, for his *open sesame* card. . . .

The two men stared as the large, blond, tired-looking man approaching them gave sudden vent to deep-throated laughter.

ABOUT THE AUTHOR

John Creasey, born in 1908, was a paramount English crime and science fiction writer who used myriad pseudonyms for more than six hundred novels. He founded the UK Crime Writers' Association in 1953. In 1962, his book *Gideon's Fire* received the Edgar Award for Best Novel from the Mystery Writers of America. Many of the characters featured in Creasey's titles became popular, including George Gideon of Scotland Yard, who was the basis for a subsequent television series and film. Creasey died in Salisbury, UK, in 1973.

THE PATRICK DAWLISH MYSTERIES

FROM OPEN ROAD MEDIA

INTEGRATED MEDIA

Find a full list of our authors and
titles at www.openroadmedia.com

FOLLOW US
@OpenRoadMedia